Seviyye Talip

MODERN MIDDLE EAST LITERATURES IN TRANSLATION

Series Editor: *Dena Afrasiabi*

Other books in this series include:

Ibn Arabi's Small Death
Poetic Justice: an Anthology of Contemporary Moroccan Poetry
The Sky that Denied Me

SEVIYYE TALIP

Halide Edib Adıvar
Translated by Iclal Vanwesenbeeck

Cover art & design by Saffron Kaplan
Book design by Allen Griffith of Eye 4 Design

Library of Congress Control Number: 2024941098
ISBN: 9781477330647

Translated from *Seviye Talip* by Halide Edib Adıvar
Copyright © 2020, Can Sanat Yayınları A.Ş.
First published in 1910

Contents

Acknowledgements

I am truly grateful to Professor İpek Hüner with whom I co-transcribed the novel from Ottoman into modern Turkish. I would also like to express my gratitude to the anonymous readers for their invaluable comments and suggestions on the translation, and the University of Texas Press editor Dena Afrasiabi for her support and contributions to the project. I live in a multilingual home, and I am forever indebted to my son and husband for joyful conversations about language and translation.

Seviyye Talip

Introduction

Halide Edib Adıvar

Few Turkish women writers have been as prolific and popular as Halide Edib Adıvar and few have been as controversial. Halide Edib was born in 1884, during the Hamidian era (1876-1909), into an affluent family. She lost her mother, Bedrifem Hanım at a very young age. Her father, Mehmet Edib Bey was one of the secretaries to sultan Abdülhamid II and was quite particular about his daughter's education. Young Halide was tutored by prominent scholars in languages, philosophy, and mathematics. She was the first Muslim woman to graduate with a degree from the American College for Girls, an American missionary school in Istanbul. At age fifteen, she co-translated John Abbot's *The Mother at Home*. A decade later, she started writing for newspapers, including the iconic Ottoman newspaper *Tanin*. Her early life as a journalist coincided with a culturally vibrant yet politically restless period in Ottoman history. She was targeted and blacklisted for her articles about women and went into voluntary exile in Egypt with her sons in 1908, only to return after the March 31 Incident that led to the deposition of sultan Abdülhamid II. It is also during this time that Halide Edib experienced marital problems. Her husband, Salih Zeki took a second wife and wanted Halide to accept the polygamous arrangement. But Halide refused it and demanded a divorce, an unorthodox move for a woman at that time. They got divorced in 1911.

Between her divorce and the beginning of World War I, Halide Edib engaged in various social, political, pedagogical, and literary endeavors. She was the founding member of the Association for the Elevation of Women, a feminist organization advocating against polygamy and for women's rights. She published a novel, *Handan* (1912), a utopia, *Yeni Turan* (1912), and an opera libretto, *Canaan's Shepherds* (1914) within the same decade, attesting to her ability to master different genres and forms. War and occupation, however, transformed Halide Edib's life and likely her artistic sensibilities. By 1919, the Ottoman Empire, having lost the war, was occupied by the allied forces, and a resistance had begun in several parts of Anatolia under Atatürk's leadership. Halide Edib and her second husband, Adnan Adıvar were among those who had joined Atatürk in the War of Independence (1919-1922). During the war, Halide Edib worked as a corporal, nurse, and war journalist. She was also the founder of the Anatolian News Agency, and a PR specialist all the while writing novels. But in the post-war period, Halide Edib and her husband went into exile after a political rift with Atatürk and were thus alienated from the political arena of the new Turkey. From 1924 until 1939, they lived in France, England, and the US, only to return a year after Atatürk's death. During this period, Halide Edib gave lectures at Barnard College, visited India as a guest of Mahatma Gandhi, and wrote relentlessly. Her two-part memoir, *Memoirs of Halide Edib* and *The*

Turkish Ordeal, as well as her globally known works such as *The Clown and his Daughter*, *Turkey Faces West* (1930), *The Conflict of East and West in Turkey* (1935), and *Inside India* (1937) were all written during her years in exile. Upon her return, in 1940, she founded the department of English Language and Literature at Istanbul University. It is in this period that she translated George Orwell's *Animal Farm* (republished in Turkey in 2021 by Fom Publishing) and co-translated several Shakespeare plays, including *Antony and Cleopatra*. After serving as an MP between 1950-54, she retired from politics. She died in 1964.

Today, excerpts from Halide Edib's works fill up Turkish dictionaries, her works are studied in doctoral theses and research projects, schools and streets are named after her; her books are required reading in Turkish high schools; and half a century after her death, books about Halide Edib still become best-sellers in the Turkish bookstores. Her two dozen works of fiction and non-fiction reveal the critical and fascinating relationship between women's writing and media, political reform, changing gender roles, justice, and a host of other critical issues central to the history of Turkey.

Halide Edib's intellectual life was certainly defined by her immaculate education, but her career as a writer was shaped by the events of the early twentieth century. These include the declaration of the second constitutional monarchy, the political uprisings of 1909, World War I, the Turkish War of Independence, and the emergence of modern Turkey. These tectonic shifts compelled Halide Edib to think about nationalism, identity, and women's rights, but also about exile and violence. Without exception, all her writings carry traces of her eventful life and offer great insight into the final years of the Ottoman Empire as well as Turkey's uneasy relationship with the West and with Westernization. Halide Edib was born into a time of war and reform, and she had a profound desire to understand the world around her and her place within it.

But at the heart of every Halide Edib story and perhaps at the heart of the Turkish question itself, are women. Until her last serialized work, *Çaresaz* (1961), we see Halide Edib writing about polygamy and women's education, and engaging in the question of who the ideal modern Turkish woman is. We see this clearly in *Seviyye Talip* (1910) as well. The novel revolves around the question of old and new, tradition and modernity, all the while making it clear that the Turkish woman marked the litmus test for reform and Westernization in the Ottoman Empire. But what makes the novel more provocative is that Halide Edib shows the reader how women are brutally objectified by even the most educated and modern of men.

I crossed paths with *Seviyye Talip* as part of a larger project on Ottoman women, opera, and literature in 2018. Much to my surprise, the turn-of-the-century Halide Edib presented different artistic and ideological sensibilities than I had anticipated. Here was an erudite woman journalist and novelist who dared to write freely about women; a writer whose exilic voice in 1908 resonated with me as modern Turkey witnessed a massive exodus of journalists and intellectuals in the 2000s. Today's Turkey, more than a century after *Seviyye Talip*, still wrestles with unprecedented cases of murder and violence against women, an increasingly xenophobic national identity, and political oppression. Halide Edib thus remains as relevant today as she was a century ago.

Seviyye Talip

"The book was published in the winter. The fact that I had dared to explore social shams and conventions brought down on my head a volley of criticism. But the book's popularity was equal to the severity of the attacks" (Halide Edib, *Memoirs*, 296).

Seviyye Talip was written between the fall of 1909 and the winter of 1910, in the months after Halide Edib returned to Istanbul from her political exile in Egypt and after a short stay in England. The 1910 edition, unlike the 1924 one, was published under her married name, Halide Salih. Halide Edib notes in her *Memoirs*, that "[she] wrote Sevie Talib during the long watches of the night" (295) as she looked after her youngest son, Hassan, who had typhoid fever.

Structurally, it might be accurate to refer to *Seviyye Talip* as Halide Edib's first novel because it is more sophisticated in character construction and structural unity than her two previous short works, *Raik's Mother* and *Heyula* (1909), and it acts as a precursor to her more popular and longer works such as *Handan* (1912) and *The Clown and his Daughter* (1935). It is worth noting, however, that in the 1910s Ottoman Empire, only a handful of women writers were publishing their work. In this regard, *Seviyye Talip* can be studied as one of the first best-selling books by an early Ottoman woman novelist. Its bold political undertones, the first-ever Ottoman soprano character in fiction, and its ambitious attempt at intertextuality make the novel and the writer especially stand out.

Seviyye Talip is divided into six parts in the 1924 edition: The Return, Scenes from the Istanbul Highlife, Futile Conflict, Heartache, Abyss, and Epilogue, and the story comprises four layers: political, ethical, historical, and artistic. The second half of the novel is written in the form of journal entries and is slightly reminiscent of Goethe's *Werther*. Aside from allusions to Paolo and Francesca, Faust and Marguerite, Shakespeare's *Antony and Cleopatra* is central to the narration of Fahir's ethical dilemma of loyalty in the novel. As Fahir's patriotism and idealism escalate, the writer introduces a threat to Fahir's idealism: Seviyye. Fahir turns her into an object of desire, but Seviyye is an honest, virtuous woman who lives for her music. She stands up against outdated values and courageously liberates herself, only to be objectified and assaulted by the allegedly reformed, modern Fahir.

Fahir spends the first two parts of the novel struggling with his infatuation with Seviyye but after a climactic exchange of lines with Seviyye from the third act of *Antony and Cleopatra*, he falls into a severe neurasthania that results in a remedial journey to Egypt. In Cairo, he meets a British primadonna, Evelyn Marshall, who is playing the role of Marguerite in Gounod's *Faust*. She falls in love with Fahir, who she thinks looks like the legendary opera composer Pietro Mascagni, but Fahir resists the temptation and returns to Istanbul. Upon his second return, he sees himself as another Antonius who leaves behind the empire for a woman and walks into his own abyss. One night, in a moment of delirium, he visits Seviyye in her home and assaults her. There is only one way left for Fahir to salvage himself from the abyss now and that is for him to become a martyr for freedom. He joins the *Army of Action* against the sultan and the novel ends with Macide and his son, Hikmet, attending the funeral prayers for the freedom martyrs.

Seviyye Talip includes major historical events of the 1908-1910 period, but it also creates a fascinating cultural landscape. Iconic buildings in Istanbul, such as the Tokatlıyan Building, Passage Petit Champs, boat rides on the Bosphorus, oxcart rides in Kayışdağı, walks on the hills of Çamlıca along with mesmerizing moments at the Cairo opera, The Shepheard Hotel, walking by the Sphinx and the pyramids, and meditative moments on the banks of the River Nile reveal more than just Halide Edib's mastery of Romantic paradigms. The linguistic, geographic, and cultural flow of the Empire is present in all these scenes, and they make *Seviyye Talip* a remarkable period novel.

A Note on the Translation

Halide Edib wrote *Seviyye Talip* in Ottoman Turkish, using a Perso-Arabic alphabet. That language is no longer in use in today's Turkey and even though there is some shared vocabulary, words are elusive in their meaning, even deceptive at times because the modern meaning of a word may have shifted from its Ottoman Turkish meaning a century ago. The original text is also laden with Persian and Arabic words, often present in any Ottoman text in this period, requiring the translator to imagine a more fluid linguistic traffic than today's Turkish and more plasticity in word construction. In this sense, translating directly from Ottoman into English meant silencing my modern Turkish and embracing an immersion in a turn-of-the-century syntactical flow and semantics. To preserve the Ottoman linguistic aspirations and to get closer to the heart of Halide Edib's word choices, I often engaged in close dialogue with Persian, Arabic, and French-Ottoman dictionaries, and spent hours imagining a word and its possible connotations. Because the novel aspires to be in dialogue with classical romances, I focused particularly on Halide Edib's Romantic lexicon, her word variations for emotions. While translating, I negotiated with the Romantic language without economizing Halide Edib's vocabulary, to give a more realistic sense of her early literary style and artistic choices.

Halide Edib was a polyglot who was in command of many languages and literary genres. However, her literary style is direct and even practical. I attribute this to her industriousness and her undying ambition to be a writer of ideas. Her expressive choices almost always favor philosophical questions or paradoxes rather than subtle metaphors. That's one of the reasons why dialogue constitutes the core of her fiction and represents a major task in translating her work. I tried to translate the dialogues as faithfully as possible, partly because she is more masterful in dialogue than in descriptive language and partly because dialogue has a more direct effect on characters who are at the crux of any Halide Edib story. I also used all her early novels in Ottoman and her three English texts, her *Memoirs* (1926), *The Turkish Ordeal* (1928) and the *Clown and his Daughter* (1935) as tonal references for my English translation. Though we may assume Halide Edib's English works received professional editing, there are also some recurring word choices in her works that inspired me in this translation. One such word she seems to have favored in her sartorial descriptions is "tattered." I adopted and kept it in my translation. In some instances, I have also emulated Halide Edib's decision to leave some Turkish words untranslated. For instance, the decision to leave the word *charshaf* is partly because she does that, too, in her memoirs. The decision to leave certain culture-specific words untranslated in the text was inspired by Halide Edib's English texts and by the wish to create a lexical space wherein the original text and the reader could meet. This brings me to the question of time, more specifically alla turca time in the novel. Although untranslated words may be easily defined in today's digitally and culturally connected world, the time and date system used in the novel requires more advanced research skills of conversion. To clarify, I would like to give two examples from the translation: the journal section and part four of the novel entitled "Futile Conflict" starts with the date September 25, 1324 in the original text. When converted to the Gregorian calendar, the date is October 8, 1908. Because the second half of the novel is in journal form and dates anchor the reader in the political events of the time, I converted the dates throughout the translation to prevent confusion about the time period of the novel. Unlike the considerable number of dates in the novel, there is a limited number of specific temporal references. In this sense, I chose not to convert or appropriate but preserved the original temporal references. Time in the early twentieth century Ottoman Empire was calculated from sunset to sunset, with an algorithm of Muslim prayers, and sunset and sunrise times. An accurate conversion of temporal references in *Seviyye Talip* is therefore not possible. For instance, in part one, "The Return," Fahir says he arrives in Numan's house at eleven o'clock. By that he means one hour before sunset, that is twelve o'clock. The twelve o'clock reference in part two, "Scenes from the Istanbul Highlife," can be translated as sunset. I hope this helps the reader orient themselves to the time of day in the novel.

For the Shakespeare lines in this translation, I used the Arden edition of *Antony and Cleopatra* and not the Oxford edition she preferred for her 1949 translation of the same play. For the Khayyam rubaiyat in the novel, I used the 1859 Edward FitzGerald English translation.

Seviyye Talip breaks tradition among Halide Edib's early works for not being serialized and sees its first book edition in 1910. The second and final edition in Ottoman Turkish was published in 1924 with minimal revisions, this time in modern Turkey, but before the alphabet reform in 1928. The original Ottoman editions of *Seviyye Talip* present the reader with a few perplexing spelling mistakes and other challenges such as the spacing of the words and different punctuation usage. All of this poses morphological challenges for the translator. In this translation, I used both the 1910 and 1924 Ottoman editions, comparing subtle changes and shifts in meaning, and tracing corrections. Where meaning was compromised due to orthographic challenges, I translated to preserve the narrative cohesion. I hope my translation does justice to Halide Edib's authorial style and tone, and her desire to share her ideas with the rest of the world.

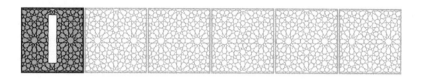

The Return

The first thing I noticed when the train stopped at Sirkeci Station was the rather tall woman in a black veil and white gloves, kindly and affectionately reaching out for the hands of the man who had run up to her from the compartment next to mine. At that moment, I deeply regretted not having told my family of my arrival in Istanbul. Now that I think about it, how petty and ignoble were my reasons for

Sirkeci Station, "Constantinople. Gare des Chemins de fer Orientaux"
Postcard, 000796. Courtesy of Atatürk Library Archives, Istanbul.

keeping the news from them. I was anxious that Macide would show up in her loose, floral charshaf, holding hands with a little boy in ill-fitting pants, and that my aunt would sneer at my friend Numan for his stylish outfit (the one I found a little over the top) with that disparaging look on her ever-stern face.

These were such trivial things, and yet three years ago, they had stung what was supposed to be my genuine happiness with invisible needles. Three years ago, I had left the country from this very station, running away from the totality of these trivial things in my life, with an obscure heaviness in my heart, looking at Macide's seventeen-year-old, child-like face, knowing the submissiveness and obedience she had in her blood, wondering why there were no tears in her still, black eyes. In these three years, I had lived a modest and quiet life in England, one that a small personal fortune could support, dedicating all my time to my studies.

Six months after I left, I had received the news of my newborn son. Macide had sent me the news in her beautiful handwriting but in an otherwise insignificant letter. In fact, every fifteen days, I received a letter from her that started and ended with the same greeting. Every now and then they would dip the hand of the child in ink and press it on the letter. But the fine details that would conquer the soul of a mother or father were absent from these letters. They had only shared the news of him saying "father" and his first steps.

I had often wondered if Macide existed beyond her meek, contumacious, and a bit shallow self. But no! For these kinds of young girls, education means knowing enough to read newspapers and write letters. They devote the rest of their time to domestic life. The most natural thing for them is to sew, tidy up, keep the rugs clean and proper, and make sure the house isn't messy. Of course, these are not things to be looked down upon, but there is also nothing in their womanhood that lures men to their warm corner. In vain you would expect to see a few bright flowers around the room; neither can you see a clean, elegant woman who is ready and willing to understand you and warm you up to the house. You arrive at home before she even has a chance to take off her work apron and as you get ready to talk to her about your ideas, her anxious eyes look for dust on the console table.

During my time in England, I stayed away from women as much as I could. Yet, I have to admit that whenever I observed social life and the lives of English women, I would get uneasy with the feeling of something missing in our nation. That's why I tried to direct my attention to other aspects of English society, ones that I thought would benefit my country. But everywhere I turned, the issue of women would rear its head and haunt me. Think of such deprivation that nothing can make up for it! It was for this reason alone that I had dedicated my time to studying philosophy. And finally, one day, when the constitutional monarchy was declared, an invisible hand from the motherland came and grabbed my heart. The need to see my country had suddenly turned England into a prison for me. I would close my eyes and see, like you would from a train window, small crowds playing with their bare feet in their tattered basma dresses, jumping in the muddy puddles in front of their houses that tightly lined up on narrow streets. I knew I had missed my country very much. I was longing to see its bright-eyed children with their small, able hands, their hard-working, patient, and weary-looking mothers who would stand at the door and call them home, and their fathers, most of whom would be in front of coffee houses, sitting in perpetual laziness. London's wide and clean streets, its magnificent buildings now looked unattractive to me compared to my country's ramshackle, cracked wooden houses.

It had been only a short while since the declaration of the constitutional monarchy. The annexation of Bosnia-Herzegovina, the independence of Bulgaria, and the Crete conflict had occurred one after the other. As I returned to work quietly in a distant corner of my homeland, a fretful and despairing cloud cast its dark shadow on that earlier, beautiful hope that the constitutional monarchy had sparked in me. I wondered if they would ever let us rebel. As I approached

The Declaration of the Second Constitution, "II. Meşrutiyet Kartpostalı, Hürriyeti Temsil eden Kadının Etrafındakiler Midhat Paşa, Prens Sabahattin, Fuat Paşa, Namık Kemal, Zinciri Kıranlar Niyazi ve Enver Beyler" Postcard, 012032. Courtesy of Atatürk Library Archives, Istanbul.

the bridge, I noticed a silent and ominous rage; a rebellion, a storm of genuine grief on people's faces, caused by the recent events. This was different from what a friend had previously described in his letter as faces "burning with euphoria, shaken to their core; excited and delirious with freedom." Later on, when I noticed how the same cloud was cast on the brows of all government officers, school-aged children, even the carriage riders and rowers, pride swelled up in my despondent soul. I thought, hearts that came together in the face of tragedy and danger, and hands uniting against the enemy were a more effective defense than any rifle and cannonball could ever be.

After I surrendered myself to the waves of the public uprising in my country, I headed home, curious about my family, wondering what my wife and aunt thought of all this. The lifeless ones in the nation who lived behind a veil of idleness and superstition! Have they finally awakened, too? Those women behind the walls, whose mundane interests are all confined to their husbands! Have they remained oblivious to their husbands' state of mind? Poor women, I thought to myself, how uninterested, how listless they were! But alas, only later in life did I realize who was actually responsible for all of this.

People had told me that after the constitutional monarchy, women were in a big fight for their rights. If you ask me, I object to causing a stir about women's rights right now. But I deem it worthy to examine men's opinions on women's rights and the course of action they will take in this matter. I happen to think that the country will be split over this: one group, the traditionalists, who will fanatically want to nip things in the bud . . . the other group, the snobs, who will want to give women endless rights *à la France*, before women receive the education necessary to make use of their freedom, or before they go through moral maturity! One side will enslave women; the other will treat her like a doll. If indeed there are some who see women as companions, as the sole mothers and educators of future generations, and want to educate them in this spirit, no doubt that these people are either the minority or the kind of people who are all words but few deeds. But what side am I on? I don't quite know. I don't have a straightforward answer to what I truly want or desire about women's rights. This wearies me like an unsolvable riddle. I guess our social conditions aren't conducive to thinking too deeply about women's rights, and this happens to be one of those delicate topics that doesn't lend itself to deeper investigation.

I got off the carriage in *Kısıklı* and started to walk. There was a faint flutter in my chest; I would see the face of my child. As I approached the house, all my mighty philosophical principles retreated. I was now returning to my homeland, which has tenaciously raised its head from all the disgrace.

When I saw the roof of our small, unpainted house, I stepped up my pace. I could hear Macide's young voice on the way. How mature she sounded. I stopped in front of the fence and listened to them:

"Mother, watch out, Hikmet will fall. Now, why would you give him börek at this hour? It'll upset his stomach."

"Allah! Allah! If it were up to you, you would starve the kid to death!"

The kitchen door was open . . . Macide was standing on the stairs, with her back turned to the garden. All those gowns that I had ordered for her; they must be sitting in a chest somewhere! On her back was a simple dress with black and white prints. The white belt around her waist helped bring out the contours of her tall body and the beauty of her young and low shoulders. Her long skirt draped over the steps. It made her neck look longer and gave her a simple perfection that one might call a classic look. Her thick, black hair was gathered at her neck in a thick braid. Her hair was uncovered; it must not have crossed her mind that any man could pass along this secluded street. She was talking to her mother who was in the kitchen, cooking. I called her name: "Macide! Macide!"

She turned at the speed of lightning. Her dark complexion blushed with surprise, joy, and hesitation. First, I thought she would storm down the steps and run towards me but instead she turned towards the kitchen, "Mother, Fahir is here!" she said to my aunt.

Then she ran down the stairs towards me. As I held Macide tightly in my arms, I could see my aunt's stern face by the kitchen door. She was dressed in her usual hand-woven kitchen apron, but this time, her eyes were tolerant and smiling. I made a gesture to run to the kitchen and greet her: "My dear aunt . . ."

But she interrupted me. "It is all right, my son, there is freedom in the country now . . ."

"Aunt! How now? Are you happy with our freedom?"

She had already gone back to her cooking pot."What is freedom to women, my son?" she said, "Let men think about it!"

Before I could feel offended by what she was saying, I noticed a child with brown hair, sitting on a highchair, watching us curiously and a little shyly from the corner of the kitchen. A minute later, he was struggling to get out of my arms, crying at the top of his lungs.

My aunt came to the rescue. "My boy doesn't know his father yet . . . Hikmet, look, this is your father!"

All three of us, overly concerned in a funny way, tried to calm Hikmet down by doing all kinds of tricks. But in the end, my tiepin accomplished what none of us could, and Hikmet eventually came to the arms that so very much longed for him.

When I woke up, Macide wasn't next to me. Hikmet was holding his pink feet in between his hands and pulling his toes resolutely, one by one. In a little distance, I saw Macide. She was sitting by the Ottoman brazier in her white night gown, taking something out of a snow-white coffee set cautiously and slowly; her thick braid hanging on her back. Once in a while, she pushed away the little curls on her forehead, but her entire attention was directed at the coffee, making sure it didn't overflow. s

"I guess this is for me."

"Indeed. I was making it for you."

She poured the coffee into the cup with utmost care and brought it to my bed.

"Why don't you and I take the boy and head out to *Beyoğlu* today?"

"What for?"

"To dress you up in new clothes that are worthy of the glory of your new freedom!"

Macide turned red: "It is not like I don't have any clothes. I was cleaning the house yesterday. That's why I had that basma dress on me."

"I know that but I feel like spending some money on you."

In the end, Macide, Hikmet, and I headed out to *Beyoğlu* that day.

As she was putting on her charshaf, Macide turned to me anxiously. "It looks ugly, doesn't it, because I don't have it fluffed up on my forehead?"

"No," I said. "I wouldn't exchange that braid curled up at the back of your tiny head or the hair that curls around your forehead, none of it, for a hairdo done by a Parisian hairdresser."

She turned her head and looked at me with grateful, bright eyes. I believe these very words proved to be the key to her agreeable and contented demeanor that day. But the minute we saw the vendeuses in Karlman walking around with their big hair, their big breasts coming out of their corsets, and their shiny red cheeks, that line between Macide's eyebrows, the one that I was just getting to know more about, that inquisitive and irresolute line, appeared. After waiting for alterations for a couple of hours, we loaded up the bags filled with Macide's blouses, fabrics for her skirts, and clothes for Hikmet.

As we were leaving the shop, she started talking contemplatively, as if something was bothering her. "I am glad that you don't like big hairdos either. If only you knew. Nowadays, even women who go out on the streets with their tattered charshaf and torn shoes get hair extensions from *Beyoğlu* and put them on their heads. Just recently, our neighbor begged me to go to the theater with her; you had to see what it was like in there."

As she opened up her heart and mind to me, she went on talking with a youthful, sincere, and joyful smile on her face. "The theatre boxes were full of women whose heads looked like castles with tons of artificial curls and meters of ribbon rising on their heads."

I could not keep myself from smiling at her last sentence.

"Have mercy, my dear Macide, I said. Not everyone has tons of naturally beautiful hair like you. And besides, some faces need extravagant hair to look more beautiful."

"All right, but, how about women who don't even have money to buy new shoes? Do you think they know what they are doing when they follow the latest hair fashion?"

"That is also true but then there are also women who walk around in their messy hair and shabby clothes. There has to be a middle ground in all of this."

Macide didn't respond. And in the meantime, we had already arrived at the pier.

There are some things that she just listens to without ever responding. I never quite understand if she keeps silent because she disagrees with what I say or if she just doesn't understand it. Last night, I talked to her about what freedom means for the country, about the new duties that fell on the shoulders of women. Once again, she kept quiet and prepared Hikmet for bedtime.

After this three-year separation, I feel as if my thoughts and feelings towards Macide are changing, that I feel growingly more enchanted by her earnest, dignified character, and her beauty. But I have one small concern. I believe she harbors a stubborn conservatism in her nature. I am willing to accept that, but I fear that it might be a deeply rooted fanaticism. The service my transforming homeland expects of me reveals itself on the faces of Macide and Hikmet. Maybe the future holds schools, free ideas, and sound opinions for the next generations of women and will pave the road for their education, but for now the

Oriental Beauties, "Meşrutiyet Hanımları, Beautes
Orientales. Costume Moderne Ancien Costume,"
Postcard, 001157. Courtesy of Atatürk Library
Archives, Istanbul.

biggest mission for educated young men like us is to awaken the current
generation of women at home, call them to action on things that will
properly equip them for life and be beneficial to the evolution of the
nation. You see, I involuntarily side with women. I have to admit that
Macide's beauty has a lot to do with this.

I spend all my time reading and talking to Macide and I cannot help but feel as if I take on the role of the teacher in our relationship. I notice something in her that I believe represents the characteristics of most women of her kind and that is, she doesn't have a clear understanding of what homeland means. Rather, she divides the world into two, as the Christian world and the Muslim world. I have talked to her extensively about this matter. I have told her that the idea of a homeland and religion are not related to each other, that a Greek-Ottoman or an Armenian-Ottoman could love their homeland as much as a Turk, or a Muslim-Ottoman. I told her that in the future, we needed to instill in our children this way of thinking, too. She listened for a while and then nodded, dissatisfied.

"All right" she said, "Let's say I accept everything you tell me, but I am afraid that this may mean soon you'll make me believe in things that go against what I have believed in since I was a child."

Two months after my return, Numan paid me a visit. He lives in *Rumelihisarı*. He said he was getting married soon and invited Macide and me to the wedding. He kept talking about how normally his mother would bring the invitation but because he didn't have one, he had to come and invite us himself. All the while, he was watching me with curious eyes.

Numan and I have been friends since our school years; we are more like brothers. He is a good fellow but a bit too Europeanized. That's why he struck right away with the question:

"Well, aren't you going to let me see your madame? It's a family wedding. You will both attend, husband and wife, right?"

"Wait here; let me ask Macide. Her opinions don't quite align with yours and mine . . ."

"But tell her that I am closer to you than a brother."

I went straight to our bedroom. Macide was waking Hikmet up from his afternoon nap. The child was acting up. He was pulling his mother's hair, kicking, and whining. Despite Macide's pleas, this little tyrant, who thought of himself as the absolute ruler of the house, got more and more out of control.

"Let go of your mother's hair," I said with a firm tone.

At that moment, I saw a little insolence and surprise in Hikmet's blue eyes. But he continued to misbehave, crying even more wildly and forcefully than before. I walked to him, grabbed his arms, took him to the corner of the room, and left him there.

"Until you decide to be a good boy and kiss your mother's hand, you will stay here."

The astonishment in Macide's eyes wasn't any less than in Hikmet's. But with all her body and soul, she sided with this little rascal who tyrannized her.

"Is this supposed to be a European style of upbringing?"

The minute Hikmet noticed the obliging look on his mother's face, he started crying at the top of his lungs. I realized that I was either going to establish my definite authority over my wife and son or that I would forever remain a weak husband and an ineffective father.

I lifted up Hikmet and put him in my office, next to my bedroom. I closed the door and repeated my first sentence. "You are here until you kiss your mother's hand . . ."

There was Hikmet, crouching on the carpet. He had surrendered the minute he was left alone in the room and was weeping quietly.

"I will kiss my mother's hand . . ."

Hearing this, Macide ran up to him eagerly and wrapped the little bandit in her arms. This was the first time I saw her scowl at me with piercing, angry eyes.

"Macide, my dear, actually, I had come in to tell you something important," I said and told her about Numan's visit.

Pretending to look busy as she put on the boy's shoes, she said, "Let me tell you, Fahir! I am a Turkish girl. I haven't lived in England like you. I cannot consort with men like European women do, with my hair uncovered." It was hard to tell if this was a sincere response or whether she said these things in a moment of anger.

"Who tells you to consort with men you don't know? I am only asking because Numan is like a brother to me. Besides, his wife will consort with me."

"She can do that if she wants to," Macide answered in an angry tone. "Who knows what kind of a coquette she is . . . Probably one of those new freedom girls . . . but I am a Turkish girl, a Muslim girl. I don't put up with any of that . . ."

I, too, was about to lose my temper and yet I still tried to show restraint and tell her, as gently as I could, how embarrassing it would be to confess to Numan her feelings about their invitation. But Macide was now entirely out of control. "I knew it. You stay in Europe for a few years and turn up your nose at us. If you have had enough of my ignorance and uncouthness, then attend the wedding by yourself.

I cannot go there to become everyone's laughingstock. I am sure you can find a woman after your own heart there."

Now, considering all my good intentions in the last two months, this was unfair. I guess I said a few rude things to her in return. Perhaps I, too, was being unfair for ignoring her feelings? And yet, here we were. What was I going to tell Numan now? I left the room with unprecedented bitterness in my heart towards Macide. I went back to Numan and told him that Macide had a headache and that she would attend the wedding if she felt better, and if not, I would be there by myself. Numan looked convinced when he left. I, on the other hand, was disappointed at the limits of my will power and goodwill, and went back to Macide's room feeling a bit regretful.

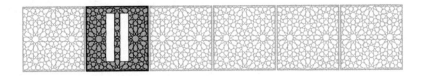

Scenes from the Istanbul Highlife

had not been able to persuade Macide to attend the wedding, and I suspected my mother-in-law had a hand in this. Since our first and last fight, Macide often visits with her mother downstairs. A few times, I caught them in my aunt's dining room; they were sitting on the woven floor cushions, chatting. One time, I overheard a conversation between them that ended abruptly as I walked in. The only thing I was able to hear was my aunt repeating her warning: "Don't even think about it! There would be no turning back . . ."

In the end, no matter how much I tried, Macide did not attend the wedding. Three days after the wedding, the hosts organized a lovely dinner party as a kind gesture to us. Yet again, everything I said about this event fell short; Macide's fierce and insecure eyes made it clear that she did not want to go to the dinner party. Finally, she said: "Looking at how much you insist on going; one would think you have something to gain by attending. If you are curious about Numan's wife then go by yourself . . . Maybe you'll find yourself a European mistress there, one you may need in the future . . ."

I wonder if Macide is jealous of these kinds of people. Does she really think I am some kind of a snob who would sacrifice his household and principles for a few French words? I feel like we, the current generation, who will popularize the values of Western civilization, carry a great responsibility. We have to be as white as snow, as innocent and pure as children. In fact, we must even surpass the old generation in our firm stance against the slightest human vice so that we can introduce new ideas and new principles to our country. But I don't think I yet understand Macide well enough. No matter how much I tried to reconcile with her in the last few days, I sadly felt defeated by my anger every time. Finally, on the day of the dinner party, I just got dressed and left without repeating my pleas. When she dusted my coat at the door, I could feel her serious-looking, still, black eyes, waiting to meet mine, hesitantly and inquisitively.

First, I had lunch at Tokatlıyan, then I walked around for a few hours trying to find a proper gift for the bride. I had planned to go to *Hisar* with the ten o'clock ferry but the afternoon hours went by slowly. My mind was on my family life. Despite my attempts and efforts to improve things, I feel as if there are more rough edges to be tolerated than can be smoothed at home.

I took the ten o'clock ferry as planned and at eleven, I found myself standing in front of Numan's prodigious, white yalı. I was greeted by a butler in a Redingote at the door who then asked a rosy-cheeked servant in a black dress, a white bonnet, and a white apron, to escort me upstairs.

Hotel Tokatlıyan, "Hotel M. Tokatlian. Grand Rue de Pera—Constantinople"
Postcard, 010838. Courtesy of Atatürk Library Archives, Istanbul.

Even before I arrived in the main hall, I could hear the voices of the
young girls talking openly and eagerly to each other. Numan's belly
laughs, and his father's perfectly constructed sentences, à la Bab-ı Ali
greetings of the court, all echoed in the hallway. Haşim Bey came to
the door, wearing his monocle, and accepted me into the main hall.
Behind his father, who had given me the most formal and graceful
welcome, was Numan, sticking his tongue out at me. As soon as his
father walked away, he came to introduce me to a child-like, petite
blonde in a white dress, as his wife. I went on to greet Numan's
sisters, Semiha and Nazlı. I had known them since we were children.
A little later, they introduced me to Numan's cousin; a tall, beautiful
brunette whose pleasant yet serious demeanor reminded me of
Macide. In little less than half an hour, a few others, including distant

relatives, close friends, five or six young women, and a few men with thin moustaches and empty looks (they could barely turn their necks in those stiff white shirts) also arrived in the main hall. By twelve o'clock, all the guests had arrived. Everyone eagerly tried to get acquainted and socialize until dinner time. The young bride was holding the hem of her long, white skirt, and walking among the guests, conversing with them, trying her best to fulfill her duties as a host. In the distance were two young brunette girls chatting with lively hand gestures. The two young men with skinny legs, pink faces, and small white hands, standing next to Numan's sisters also seemed to be in a deep conversation. And a skinny, young girl with a dark complexion and messy hair was talking about something in exaggerated and artificial gestures. Up close, Haşim Bey, Numan, and the bride were laughing, having a good time. Numan's young cousin, on the other hand, was sitting all by herself in the corner. I could sense that despite her solemn and regal appearance, she wasn't used to this lifestyle, that she felt like an outsider, that she was self-conscious and perhaps feared she would do something ridiculous to embarrass herself. There was something in her still, chestnut eyes, her exaggerated hairdo (likely styled by her cousins) that reminded me of Macide. I immediately went to sit next to her. At first, she was puzzled, shy and hesitant, and stuttered when answering my questions, but in time, she got used to my presence. None of the snobs in the main hall bothered to interact with this timid, new girl. I could hear shreds of their conversations around me filling the room:

"Ma chère, I am following the new political party affairs with a serious *passion*."

"I don't fancy politics. Nimet's dress doesn't do it for me. But then when was the last time tailor Kalivrosi was successful?"

"Excuse me, my dear, but even Spiegel doesn't have the chic flair Kalivrosi adds to his evening dresses."

"No way; I will protest if you say anything about Spiegel. He is the one and only *comme il faut* dressmaker in Istanbul."

"*Mon cher*, I made such a gaffe in *Hariciye* the other day! Listen, it is about Nazır Pasha."

"How about Madam Süha's latest scandal . . ."

Laughter, whispers, expressions of surprise in French continued to resonate in the air while my friend, this young girl, listened admiringly yet enviously to how people could use French phrases so naturally. Finally, it was time for dinner, so we headed to the dinner table. Numan's wife was on my arm, talking in a high-pitched voice like a chirping canary. I was trying to analyze how this unsophisticated but graceful, good-hearted but spoilt woman and Numan acted towards each other. It strikes me as one of imitation; copied from European-style friendships rather than being a serious love affair or romance.

As the night went on, I became increasingly thankful that Macide had decided not to attend the dinner party. However meaningless and innocent a gathering this was, it was a poor imitation of the genuine Western lifestyle that I so wanted to attract her into. I knew that if she were here tonight, unlike Numan's cousin who watched all of this covetously, Macide's silent but dignified, perceptive eyes would crush this society under a bitter and scornful gaze.

My conversation with Numan's wife about my son Hikmet at the table was suddenly interrupted by Numan's authoritative voice: "I forbid you to say anything against Seviyye Talip."

Suddenly, all eyes turned to Numan. His face had turned red, aflame with anger. That petite, superficial girl next to him, the one with the messy hair, was staring at Numan's wife with a mocking and suggestive glance. Next to her was the man whom they had introduced to me as the husband of one of the cousins. He was wearing a high collar shirt and had rosy cheeks and high eyebrows. He was looking around with a ridiculous expression, unsure whether to laugh or get angry. A young man on our side of the table interrupted in a weary, arrogant tone:

"To be honest, it is not even proper to utter her name in the company of ladies . . ."

"You are wrong," Numan retorted. "Seviyye Talip is as respectable as any other name, worthy to be uttered in the company of any honorable woman. I will never allow for anyone to insult her that way."

"Well then, I must say, I really pity all those years you have spent in England."

"Don't pity my years in England. Instead, pity yourself. Pity your own hypocrisy, your shortsightedness, how you could turn a blind eye to all kinds of deception but attack a woman who stood up against tradition and is, in reality, as virtuous—do you understand—as your sisters and your wives. Rest assured that an Englishman would act quicker than I against such an insult toward a woman whom he knows to be virtuous."

Numan's father interrupted him anxiously. This kind man who could not give up the old ways of Turkish hospitality spoke in a firm voice: "Numan, you are forgetting that you are the host. Let's change the subject."

But Numan was still furious. He started to speak again: "But Father . . ."

"There is no but. If I wanted to, I would have defended my own brother's wife. Enough now . . ."

A chilling silence covered the air and once again Numan's father was at work, trying to break the silence with his one-of-a-kind politeness, and it looked like he was succeeding. I, on the other hand, was trying to trace the vague memories that Seviyye's name had evoked in me. I was trying to remember her. The name sounded so familiar. I eventually decided to ask Numan's wife.

"Who is this Seviyye Talip?"

"You don't know her? She is Numan's aunt, Talip Bey's wife."

"Now I remember. Tell me, why isn't Talip Bey's wife here? And why did this woman's name cause such a stir in the room?"

We had to leave the table before I could get an answer from Numan's wife. The guests were enjoying their coffee in the warm and well-lit corners of the main hall. They seemed to have already forgotten about the argument downstairs. Reclining idly on their chairs, in their post-dinner languor, they looked entirely at peace with the world around them. Only Numan still looked upset. His wife watched him from a distance with a thin, anxious line between her eyebrows, but before long, she joined the crowd gathered around the most cheerful guest in the room, the girl at the piano. For a young girl her age, she played quite well. Then she started singing a piece (I couldn't remember which one) by Chaminade in a high-pitched and somewhat pretentious voice. Right in the middle of the song, she turned her piano bench towards Numan, who was smoking quietly in the corner, and said, "Seviyye Talip should have been here to sing this song." in a mocking and victorious tone. Numan was about to respond but after throwing her a cold, contemptuous look, he continued on with his cigarette.

It was now four o'clock. I had to leave since I had promised Macide that I would return home with the six o'clock ferry from *Beşiktaş*. Numan walked with me to the gate. I shook his hand more firmly than ever and left. Tonight, I had seen a new side to my carefree, fashionable yet shallow friend Numan.

As I was changing ferries and afterwards on the bumpy ride back home, my mind was occupied with a single name, a single face from the past, trying to fill in the blanks. I remember . . . my mother was still alive back then, and we were living in *Feneryolu*. I had just become friends with Numan, who lived next door. Our mothers had decided to enroll both of us at Sultaniye after much deliberation. I recall how important we both felt the first time we came back home in our school uniforms. All of a sudden, it felt like we were five, six years older; and more mature. The first thing we did after greeting our mothers was to run to our neighbor and friend, Ahmet Bey's daughter, little Seviyye, and ask what she thought of our uniforms. Yes, I do recall Seviyye quite well now; with her short dress and the features that distinguished her from everyone else. She was a sedulous girl who loved boys' games and physical activity as much as any boy. Despite the uneasiness and shyness boys our age felt around girls, Seviyye never made us feel uneasy. We had instantly become friends. She had a skinny British governess with glasses and thick-heeled shoes. The minute she completed her lessons with the governess, Seviyye would run to Numan's garden and jump the rope with her thin legs and quick steps. I guess she wasn't that fond of books and serious subjects because whenever her governess appeared with a book in her hand, on her way to *Fener*, and called out her name in the middle of our game (with an English that she hummed through her big teeth), Seviyye used to respond to her grumbling governess with a perfunctory "yes, yes." She never really wanted to leave the game. But then she would eventually obey this wrinkly old woman like a little lamb and go with her, albeit dragging her feet.

I remember that they would often make her wear a short blue dress with a scoop-front neckline. She had a big, round, and rather pale face over her pale neck which older men would sometimes stare at rather strangely. Maybe it was the combination of her somewhat long nose, the pale and thick lips covering her white teeth, her brown brows, eyelashes, and blonde hair that ended up creating a certain colorlessness on her face and made her look not so charming. But whenever she lifted her eyelids covering her downcast gaze, her dark chestnut-colored, versatile, big, sincere eyes would smile at you. When we played together, I would always resort to childish tricks to make those pale eyelids go up and reveal what was inside. Her eyes were like gems of beauty that had wondrous, unpredictable effects on others. Besides all this, I recall her big and strong hands, plump palms that led to slim fingertips and pinkish fingernails. Those chestnut eyes, palms, and fingernails were the only colors on this child who otherwise looked cold in her amorphous paleness and would therefore grab every stranger's attention.

There is one more face in my memories of Seviyye's childhood, and it is Haşim Bey's brother, Talip Bey. He was a teacher in Sultaniye back then. I remember his thin, black moustache, big black eyes, red lips, graceful and handsome face. I'll never forget the time when my mother and I spent a few days at Numan's house during the month of Ramadan. One night, Ahmet Bey and Seviyye had joined us for iftar and afterwards took all of us out to see an Italian opera company, (whose name I cannot recall) in *Beyoğlu*. Haşim Bey and Talip Bey had also joined us.

Because it was my first time at the opera, I was overwhelmed, rather hypnotized with the opera stage: the men in costumes, talking to each other in songs, the stylish women, the lights, sparkling diamonds, all of it, really. I didn't know which opera it was. I guess that night's program was a mixed one. With every song, Talip Bey charismatically uttered the name of the piece: "*Cavalleria Rusticana*, from the first act," he would say; "*Paillase*; ah, and this one is *La Boheme*, what a marvelous piece this one is! And they added arias from *Aida* in this . . ."

I remember Seviyye, spellbound, watching Talip Bey with reverent eyes. But the truth was she knew about opera as much as Talip Bey. There she was in front of the opera box, singing along with her favorite tunes like a nightingale, moving her fingers on an imaginary piano. After all, Seviyye's talent for music, the beauty of her voice and her

Petits Champs Theatre, "Théâtre et Amphithéâtre Municipal des Petits
Champs, Constantinople" Postcard 004531, Courtesy of Atatürk Library
Archives, Istanbul.

absolute ear were well known in the family. I, on the other hand,
with the innocence and desires of a thirteen-year-old, had fallen in
love with the half-naked primadonna. I was consumed by the way she
was singing, how she bent forward, stretched her hands out tragically
towards the audience, opened her lips, her voice soaring in those
dizzying high notes. I was quivering and my whole existence had
obediently and passionately surrendered to the primadonna's voice.

When we returned to Haşim Bey's house that night, each of us lost
sleep over different things. I was thinking about the primadonna's
tragic laughter, naked shoulders, how she rolled her big eyes encircled
with glitter and black kohl. Numan was still humming the tunes; the
old folks were cold and hungry, and Talip Bey looked contemplative.
Only Seviyye was wide awake. On that pale face—which matched

the long, white coat and white head cover—her usual half-closed eyelids were wide open. With sweet and dark sparkles, they revealed a different kind of attraction, a different kind of meaning, a different kind of beauty.

As soon as she arrived at the house, Seviyye had gone straight into the dining room, next to the selamlık, and without even taking off her head cover, she had started imitating the sopranos we watched that night, making the o-shaped mouth, singing arias. "Don't even try, Seviyye." I said to her, "You cannot sing like that primadonna in the blue dress."

"In the blue dress? Oh, you mean the primadonna without a blue dress. And, what do you mean I cannot sing like her? What that sunken-eyed, ugly woman sings is nothing."

"Excuse me. Why would she be sunken-eyed? She was the most beautiful of all."

Numan was chuckling. Showing off his beloved French, he said: "This . . . The one with the blue dress was a *fleur fanée*, the one with the pink dress was so *fraîche*, so pretty."

"Not at all."

"Ask my Uncle Talip if you don't believe me."

Without hesitation, Seviyye sided with Numan and started imitating my primadonna in a silly manner. With her hands on her diaphragm, trying to extend her small body forward, making that o-shaped mouth, her eyes exuding life and joy, she announced "Cavalleria Rusticana."

Upon hearing Seviyye's voice, all the adults came into the room, quietly lined up in front of the door, and started listening to her. Her face, initially full of life from the convulsions of genuine laughter, slowly took on a grave expression with the effect of the music and blossomed with rapture. At one point, as she breathed out the notes like a tragic cry with trembling lips and gleaming eyes; her voice carried such a heavy and divine lovelornness that we all stood there, spellbound by this child's might and spell. She, on the other hand, as if her little heart could not take any more of the mysterious sufferings and had overflown, suddenly started sobbing on the chair.

We all ran up to her, worried. Her father, who yielded to all her wishes, tried to wipe her tears, and stroked her hair gently. Numan emptied out his pockets, ready to give all his chocolate to her. Haşim Bey promised her a big baby doll. But amidst the crowd, there was one quiet person who looked as sad as Seviyye, and that was Talip Bey. The fervor and impact I saw on that baby face of his had taken me by surprise. But that night, only he had succeeded to calm Seviyye down.

That summer, Seviyye did not want to hang out with any men and after two- or three-years' time, she and Talip Bey were married. As soon as they got married, this young couple retreated to a small house they purchased in *Pendik*. For the last twelve years, whenever anyone needed to hear of a lasting love story defined by loyalty and passion, Numan would tell me of his uncle's love for Seviyye. Now I wonder what had changed this woman's enduring virtue and loyalty? What had happened to her?

As I traveled in time, going back ten, fifteen years, stirring the depths of the past, following the intertwining threads of my memories, I had forgotten all about Macide. As the carriage, which I had taken out of the barn with such difficulty, brought me closer to the house on a bumpy ride, I kept thinking back on the lives of others, the infirmity and tragedy that exiled the name of a woman I knew in childhood from society, and a thousand other unresolved feelings and thoughts, all of which made me think of Macide with a caring affection. As soon as I arrived, I jumped out of the carriage and in the numbing dampness of the cold night, I quickly passed by the garden and the kitchen stairs. The peasant woman who had been cooking in our house since I returned from London came to the kitchen door, half-asleep, wearing her headscarf, and holding a small kerosene lamp. The absolute serenity in the house shook my soul with a strange sense of loneliness. I don't know why but I had imagined I would see Macide on the other side of the door. I passed by my aunt's room but it was quiet; my aunt was praying. When she saw me at the door, she recited "Allahu akbar" quickly; I waited a little, then she went on to recite the salaam and ended her prayer.

At first, she stared at me with forbidding eyes, then she pointed upstairs with her hand and said: "Macide is waiting for you."

I was taken aback by the threatening and scornful tone I sensed in her voice. It was as if her eyes were saying, "Wait until you see what Macide will do to you," implying an already decided upon quarrel or chastisement. I hoped deep inside that she didn't do anything to make things worse between Macide and me because I had never felt as compassionate, loving, and understanding toward Macide as I did that night.

I took the stairs slowly. The bedroom door was half open and there was light inside. I tiptoed into the room. The scene in front of me melted my heart. Macide had fallen asleep with her head resting on

Hikmet's small bed. Her soft, black, wavy hair, adorning her shapely head, was tousled. On her small, elegant face sat a childish sorrow. Her pink lips were half open; one of her hands had fallen to her side, the other one grabbing Hikmet's bed. I approached her quietly and lifted her head up towards me. She suddenly opened her eyes. She looked conflicted as if she couldn't decide whether to remember the source of her anger from a long time ago or wrap her arms around me tenderly. I pulled her young face into my arms. No other night had we gotten along so well.

After that day, I noticed in her a sincere interest in my views, and an effort and determination to look modern. She even came out to sit with Numan and his wife that week, and didn't show any of her stubborn fanaticism or voice those naïve ideas she harbored underneath that dignified silence of hers. But every now and then, her childhood, her nature and nurture would bestir, because of my aunt, and in those moments, she would act distant and rebellious, and turn a vindictive and cold shoulder to me, as if I'd forced her to commit the worst sin. How hard I tried to warm her up to reason and smooth out her sharp corners. On the other hand, I was happy that she didn't throw out her old principles and her way of thinking like they were old clothes; that she didn't mindlessly accept every new thing that came her way. Macide was serious, firm in her ideas. It was her reasoning that was not right. If she could be trained to feel properly and see properly, no doubt she could be one of the much-needed types of women in this time of crisis. My involvement in Macide's education of ideas was therefore built on the principles of national and social need, as well as experience. This is the kind of progress that starts with those who are trapped between the walls and who, at the same time, will determine the future of the upcoming generations.

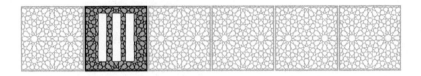

Seviyye Talip

My aunt returned from Istanbul. Her carriage arrived right when Samime and Numan were leaving our house. Numan and I were already good friends and now, a new friendship had blossomed between Samime and Macide, despite their different personalities. But my aunt was not content with this scene. When she saw me walk Samime to their carriage, and Macide see off Numan at the kitchen door, she was infuriated. Fuming, she passed by us and walked up to her room without greeting anyone.

That night, at the dinner table, all hell broke loose. My aunt was furious; why was I such close friends with Numan; why were we allowing our wives to socialize with other women's husbands? Eventually, she lost control and yelled: "You can be a monsieur, but I cannot turn my daughter into a madame!"

Hikmet was upset from all the yelling. I grabbed him from his highchair and stormed off from the table.

"If you don't like the way I behave then I'll take my wife and leave."

She finally let go of the tears she'd held back in her rage: "Look at this rascal now! He intends to separate me from my only child at my old age!"

I got away from her, but Macide, who looked guilty by association, melted away with her mother's tears. My latest outburst against her mother, whom she had obeyed in everything since the cradle, had really hurt her. Sad and confused by the hostility between the two people she loved so much, she retreated to a corner. Besides not being able to keep my calm during these increasingly frequent quarrels, I also wanted to get away from this life of constant fighting. That's why I decided that once Macide was less emotional, I was going to suggest that we leave my aunt's house and move into our own place. If I could make her accept this, I would have the upper hand and Macide would quickly become the kind of woman I want her to be. But I needed to convince her, a woman so very devoted to her mother . . .

With the uneasy thought of future fights with Macide, I grabbed my walking cane and hurtled out to the street. I walked along the *Küçük Çamlıca Road* as the cool, white mist of the moonlit sky spread on the horizon, over the mountains, all the way into my soul. My lonely heart had never felt this forlorn before. I wondered if I would feel this lonely had Macide and I lived on our own, with no obstacles in our way? It was hard to tell but what I knew was that this beautiful, black-haired woman and I didn't fully belong to each other. This revelation, on that dream-like *Çamlıca Road*, filled me with both a sense of freedom and a strange sadness.

The streets were empty. There was a foreboding silence in the illuminated sky, filled with various shades of white smoke spreading towards *Kayışdağı* and *Marmara*. I wondered if the truth we needed so desperately descended on our souls from the heavens in moments like this. With a strange and captivating yearning, I stopped there and waited. Before long, a sublime voice, falling from the white clouds, echoed on the white-capped tips of the dream-like mountains. I wasn't sure what she was singing but the mesmerizing and sublime harmony, the waves of notes pouring out of her soul could make one forget oneself. This was such a profound, such a divine voice of heavenly joy and happiness that it touched your heartstrings.

I collapsed to my knees right there on the white road, and simply listened to this voice. This was such delicious, fine ecstasy that even after the singing was over, her voice resonated mightily for a while in my ears, in my soul, in my entire existence. I don't remember how long I stayed there but when I was ready to go back, I knew I wanted to get away from all the everyday conflict and tension of the past few months. I just wanted to surrender to the uninhibited pleasures of sensations and live.

When I returned home, I found Macide weeping, exhausted from Hikmet's daylong tantrums. But my heart was filled with the mystery of the voice that echoed with a solemn intoxication of love in the white night. I passed by the narrow stairs, the dark hallway, the messy crib, and the troubles of this nervous and weary woman and went straight to bed. As I watched the light dashing on my window, I felt a burning desire to know the woman whose voice had entranced me for hours.

The next morning, I woke up in quite a relaxed mood even though I was determined to break off all relations with my aunt the night before. I felt rather inclined to get along and reconcile with everyone. My aunt looked calmer but more vengeful. The next day, she left for her sister-in-law's house in Istanbul for a week. I rejoiced at the thought of her absence, thinking that Macide and I would enjoy some privacy and freedom, but I was wrong. Macide's attitude towards me had changed because of all the innuendos and deceit. She was sulking at me, with a doubtful, reproaching gaze. That night, when I grabbed my walking cane to go to the countryside, her attitude became more pointed. She yawned and started getting ready for bed in a chilling silence. How I foolishly thought she would offer to come along. I resented the fact that despite all my care, she could still be so easily swayed by others. I left home without saying a word to her.

That night, there were only a few clouds in the sky. The moonlight, rather than spreading across the canopy like last night, was rather like a silvery spring flowing amongst the black lines and half-dark shadows; a leaden beam of light that dived into the cavities of the mountain. Once in a while, a breeze swelled up from the earth to the clouds, beating my shoulders and wrapping around my body, then vanished into the darkness. I pulled myself back in fear. Suddenly, a woman in white emerged from the bushes and onto the road.

She was of average height but strongly built. Under the moonlight, her wide face looked as white as her headscarf. As she headed towards the dark side of the road, she looked like a fleeting specter disappearing into the dark. Suddenly, she turned her head and with a voice that I desperately wanted to recognize, said, "Cemal, let's go to our piano!" Then a small man dressed in black, slowly descended onto the road and joined her, wrapping his hands around her waist, gently and gallantly. They slowly walked away. A loving, agreeable couple! My God, this was the life of others! How they could be united in heart and spirit, and shed all of life's petty resentments, all those trivial things that weighed heavy on the heart!

A female voice waltzed up into the air the way a virtuoso's bow dances on the violin. I immediately recognized it; it was that same voice from last night. There was something about this voice that meandered idly, unsure of which feeling or state to land on. Sorrowful, reserved, affectionate, wrathful: which ineffable key in the human heart was she singing of? It was hard to tell . . . The couple walked on and I kept following them. They turned right, before reaching *Çilehane*. They were surely going into that small house that nested behind the green bushes. After about ten minutes, I could hear the piano. The harmony, the melodies in the air flowed into my heart like the mighty flow of distant oceans, filling it with awe and veneration. The tempting and defiantly happy voice from last night had left its place to a solemn, lamenting, and commanding voice. This was an aria from *Aida*. She started singing, "Ah! pietà! Che più mi resta? Un deserto è la mia vita." I knelt down, hearing all the phases of a divine tragedy in my very soul. This voice . . . how easily it could take the human soul through an emotional journey with just the slightest change in tone. I returned home feeling truly humbled in front of the entire world.

When I arrived home, I found a contemplative Macide in the room. She was rocking Hikmet's crib with one hand, her eyes wide open, and there was that deep line in between her eyebrows again. There was something that made this woman always so pensive and put such a thick and cold distance between us. But what was it? Tonight, I wanted to hold her young hands gently and affectionately and straighten the lines on her forehead, which I knew to be the outward reflection of her soul. I sat next to her and lifted her chin up. With all the sincerity in my heart, diving into the depths of her black and mysterious eyes, I said:

"Tell me, my woman. I would like to create, by any means possible, a true harmony, true partnership between us; reciprocity in our feelings and thoughts, but I see that I cannot succeed. Tell me, why are you so anxious? What more can I do to make you happy?"

She closed her eyes. As tears streamed through her long eyelashes, she said, "Nothing . . ." with trembling lips.

"What do you mean nothing! I can see that your heart is broken and that I might have unknowingly caused this."

"That's true but it is not merely a few things that upset me. If I say it, you will think I am insane. Besides, I don't think I have what it takes to express it. First of all, I realize that I am not the kind of woman who could be your companion. No, please don't try to stop me from speaking. I feel like the husband who came back from Europe turned out to be a different person than the cousin I married. You see and interpret everything differently. It's like when it comes to our morals, we are two rivers that flow in opposite directions. If I obey you, my mother will resent it. If I side with my mother, you will no longer love me. You wouldn't understand what it feels like, but I was raised to say yes to my mother unconditionally since childhood and I can't manage to give up that habit easily. In fact, even when I find her reasoning to be ridiculous at times, I cannot help but find myself thinking like her. I have thought about this night and day. I will lose my mind over it . . . I am beginning to think that we can no longer be . . ."

She started sobbing in my arms before she could finish her sentence. At that moment, I could see it clearly, this was the tormenting sickness that our entire nation had been plagued with: the conflict between the new and the old. On the one hand, the old that we love and are attached to through our memories, our past, our childhood! On the other, the new, our only road to the future, a road we can only pave with determination, fortitude, and perseverance! How much patience we need to move those who are undecided, who are stuck in between the old and the new, forward. Giving people the impression that we vilify our past would especially invalidate all the efforts of reformers like us. As we try to bury the old in a reverent way, we should show all the virtues of the new, its momentous, critical qualities, and how it differs from imitation. First, we must explain to everyone how modernity has nothing in common with the lamentable imitators we see around us today. A woman who is ready to adopt modernity is not going to be an exact copy of a French or English woman. The same is true for men. They will not be modeled after Parisian men. We will not just repeat what other nations do, like monkeys. We will be the evolved, new Turks, who have applied their philanthropic theories to life, accepted the progress of the West, civilized, and utterly loyal to the essence of their race. I thus talked patiently with Macide, relating all of this to her small world. I told her that accepting my ideas would not mean falling out with her mother, that she should be respectful towards her mother and yet show character, that everyone needed to have their private lives and if every child does exactly what their parents did, there could be no progress. Even after listening to all of this, she looked at me as if she were still seeking answers.

Then, burying her head on my shoulder, she said, "But that is not all I want to know. I also think that you will not love me anymore because I am so foolish."

I tried to reassure her as best as I could and told her that it wasn't so, but she was unconvinced: "I am scared that if you meet one of those new women who thinks like you that you'll fall in love with her. Thankfully, Numan's wife is still a baby!"

I laughed. Despite her ignorance and childishness, she was prescient.

After this, there was an awakening in Macide. She spent her time reading English language books, geography, history books, health pamphlets; in short, she got every new book that came out, and read whatever she could get her hands on. Especially because she tried to keep up with everything that was published during the first months of the second constitutional period, she had a newspaper in her hand even during mealtime.

Somedays, I would wake up in the middle of the night, only to find her at her study desk, which she had placed right next to Hikmet's crib, lost in thought, and looking tired. I now sought refuge in my aunt's generosity for not just my daily cup of coffee but even to have my clothes repaired. Whenever she had to sew a ripped seam on me, she would be disgruntled.

"As if she will be a teacher! What is all this to womankind any-way? I guess if they cannot find a grand vizier in the palace, they will appoint her."

"Perhaps, Aunt, dear. The way things are, it may even be your turn. We are running out of men."

"You rascal, quiet now. You have turned my daughter into a bookworm."

"I regret it too, I swear, because I can no longer see Macide either."

After I complained day and night about our messy bedroom, I finally persuaded my aunt to hire a Greek servant. And this didn't turn out to be such a bad thing after all. The servant was now the subject of all my aunt's wrath and hostility. As she kept busy with her hatred and contempt of Eleni, she forgot about her bitterness against Numan. And Numan took advantage of this and won her graces to the point where he almost camped out on my aunt's sofa. I could sometimes hear her yell at him affectionately for barging in without giving her time to cover her hair.

I was now harvesting the fruit of my recent efforts. A woman who ignores her own child so she can in earnest be a companion to me! A loving companion who is always in your house! Then come endless desires about the future!

Numan and his wife visited us during the full moon. After dinner, the four of us went for a walk on *Uzun Yol*. In the middle of the road, I remembered the beautiful voice I had heard on the last full moon. I don't know why but I made a connection between this voice and Seviyye Talip, and just like that asked Numan: "What was that all about at your wedding, the quarrel over your aunt, Seviyye Talip?"

Numan replied: "How would I know? My dad's puritanism, I guess."

Numan's wife Samime jumped in fiercely: "Your father was right, Numan. A married woman who is living with another man!"

"You have such a simplified way of saying the truth, Samime."

"Is there such a thing as embellished truth?"

Numan was getting angry: "Women only see the outward appearance of things, especially if they have a chance at tarnishing each other's names!"

Macide replied to this: "Pardon me, Numan Bey. Do tell us about the whole thing first and then let's see if all women judge her the same way."

Samime didn't give Numan a chance to speak. Her voice was shaky: "Talip Bey's wife Seviyye fell in love with her piano teacher and ran away from her husband's home and is living with him. Numan embellishes all this, and makes a scandal look like a virtue."

"Please stop for a moment and allow me to say something."

I had run out of patience. "Why would we stop, my dear Numan? Our childhood friend's tragedy makes me sad, but that's all . . . I am afraid this has gone too far. It is a subject that I would not want discussed in Macide's presence!"

Macide replied: "Fahir, you don't want it discussed in *my* presence! I am not a child! I'd like to know everything. No, mine is not just a simple curiosity. I would like to get to the heart of the matter, the truth, so I can pass my own judgment."

I was annoyed by Macide's unexpected reasoning. "I don't appreciate this much modernity, my dear Macide. Samime Hanım told us the story. Let's leave it up to the novelists to embellish it. Those who don't believe there is absolute good and evil in the world always end up with immorality."

"Oh, merci!" Numan said, "But I must insist that if I tell you the story of Seviyye Talip, you and Macide Hanım would both admire her!"

"I personally am not interested in love stories but perhaps Macide is. Go ahead."

Numan turned to Macide and pretended like Samime and I were not there. I was talking to Samime about England, but in fact, I was curious about what Numan had to say. He was telling the story so sincerely and passionately that even Samime could not help but lend her ears in admiration.

Numan started with Seviyye's childhood and the superior education that she had received: "If you had known her back then, Macide Hanım, you would not have believed in anything they say about her today. Perhaps she was not a hard-working, serious, smart woman such as yourself, but she was an innocent, honest child, free of any girl tricks, nearly a manly child. I don't recall anyone else among my friends who was as veracious as she was. Even Fahir is not an exception to this. This girl harbored ardent emotions, she had a poet in her, but she also had a man's stubbornness to live her life the right way, on her own terms."

"It's a pity that her right is considered wrong by the moralists," I said.

Without bothering to reply to me, Numan went on with his story: "But there was something else in this girl's life, a passion, and a curiosity that consumed her entirely, and that was her music. There is no doubt in my mind that if she were to take the stage today, she could be the world's greatest primadonna simply because there is no other voice that can express every pain, every joy in the human soul the way her voice can."

"You see, you are blinded by her artistic talent and cannot see the evil in her actions." I said.

"Will you be quiet, Fahir? There is certainly something I could add to the story here, but I will not. Do you really think I'd fall in love with every primadonna in a blue dress, like you do? Macide Hanım, I'll tell you about this later! Anyway, at sixteen, Seviyye married a vapid, insensitive man thinking she was in love with him."

"You are being too respectful to your uncle, Numan!" said Samime, but once again, there was no response from Numan.

He continued with his story: "She lived with this man for twelve years. No other wife could be as loyal as Seviyye was to her husband. Away from the whole world, between those walls, thinking like her husband, feeling like her husband, as if she had lost herself inside his personality. The truth is, she always hated pretense, fake friendships, and meaningless entertainments. But one day, she finally woke up from this long sleep: Her husband's personality wasn't enough to keep her alive. Also, who knows how she must have watched her exquisite dreams and beliefs vanish. There was no child either who would tie Seviyye to a man less than her and who didn't make her happy. It must be around this time that Cemal entered her life, or perhaps she just started feeling differently about Cemal, her long-time piano teacher. In short, she fell in love with him. But Uncle Talip would not have known anything about it if Seviyye didn't tell him. That was the extent of her honor and dignity. Just like that, one day, she courageously told Uncle Talip that she no longer loved him, that they could no longer be husband and wife, and asked that they separate on friendly terms. Uncle Talip responded with the rudest threats, saying he would condemn her to house imprisonment and much more. Despite his threats, Seviyye never lost her calm. She fled to her father's house at the first opportunity she had, and for six months, she led a quiet and solitary life with her father. But after a while, she stood up for herself in the name of her youth and in defense of her right to enjoy life like everyone else. She wrote to her husband that if he didn't give back her freedom, she would live together with this man and that in her conscience she considered herself a free woman. At first, she received tearful letters from Talip Bey but soon his letters turned into threats. Eventually, Seviyye's father intercepted one of the letters and read all the slander that Talip Bey had included! Seviyye left her father's house the next day and started living with Cemal. After that, Uncle Talip started following them and made sure they were kicked out of every neighborhood they lived in. And in the end, he and Seviyye had to hide their residence from everyone. But no matter what, Seviyye always had a staunch conviction in her own honor and truths! She thinks that marriage can only be built on love. You see, even in this response, which could easily tarnish the image of other women, there is such unwavering dignity. Not even a woman who has led a virtuous life for forty years in every particular detail of her lifestyle could claim such meticulous purity and chastity as Seviyye."

When Numan was done with his story, I was torn. I still could not bring myself to agree with the ideas of this woman, who dared to live a life so contrary to public belief. On the other hand, I also could not help but respect her.

"Now, I am sure Numan knows where Seviyye lives, but he is hiding it from us," Samime said, in a defeated and resentful tone.

Macide replied contemplatively, as if she didn't hear Samime: "Yes, love is the holiest matrimony. Nothing can unite two hearts other than love."

With a strange fear in my heart, I pulled Macide by her arm: "What are you saying, Macide? Are you defying all the laws of society? Are you letting marriage hang from such thin strings?"

Macide didn't say anything. She took my hand to her fast-beating heart. I don't know why but I didn't want to see this kind of fervent transition in Macide's uneventful life, even if that passion was directed towards me.

"I only say it because I am certain that I will love you until I die. But, if you ever love someone else, I will just walk away from your life."

As I listened to Macide whisper these words to me nervously, under the dream-like gleam of the moon, I shivered with the thought of a flash of light coruscating over our dark, unknown destiny.

The next day, at breakfast, Macide told me that she wanted to take music lessons.

"I wonder when you will ask to have oil painting lessons."

"Do you want to learn how to play the piano?" Numan asked.

"Without a doubt."

"But, my dear wife, you don't have a piano."

"Why, is that a problem? You can buy one."

"Certainly, my lady."

Numan and I spent the following day in *Beyoğlu*, picking out a piano for Macide, but this difficult task wasn't completed overnight. It took us a good three days. In the end, when a new Pleyel was placed across from my study desk, Hikmet and Macide, alike in their childishness, cheered at every sound that poured out of its keys. Now it was time to choose a tutor. This task, I left up to Numan who happened to be quite the expert in the field. He took a week to think it through and then one day he delivered the news: "There is only one teacher who will either teach her how to play the piano in a short time or will not even undertake the training, and that person is the piano teacher of the whole family . . ."

"And also, Seviyye's lover!" I interrupted him.

"You have become so stubborn and cold-hearted, Fahir! Seviyye considers the man you call her lover, her husband."

Truly troubled, he added: "Poor man will be out of a job if everyone continues to judge his private life like this. When he used to teach piano to all the young people in the family, we used to admire his astuteness and his mastery of the piano. Who knows how dirty the lives of the other piano teachers you will bring home may also be? If you are a hypocrite, sir, they will forgive you in this country, even for the worst moral crimes, but heaven forbid you dare to think differently than everyone else. Now that, they will never forgive."

"That's more than enough, Numan. Come on! Find Cemal Bey and find out his fee for piano lessons, twice a week, then come back and let me know."

With his usual cheerfulness, Numan threw his arms around my neck and rushed out.

Macide was taking piano lessons from Cemal two times a week now. I used to run into Cemal at Numan's house or his relatives' house, so I was already acquainted with him. He was a small, blonde Hungarian convert in his forties. He led a solitary life, and was quiet, and I guess a bit haughty, too, since there reigned in the cold gaze of his icy, blue eyes, some contempt towards people. Cemal Bey was a little guarded, an undiscovered but much-respected musician. How I was endlessly curious about this man now. I wanted to know what Seviyye found in this quiet, middle-aged man.

On the days Macide had her piano lesson with Cemal Bey, I often had to work at my desk, across from the piano, and I watched Cemal with probing eyes during these hours: How much difference there was between this man and Talip Bey. The latter had broad shoulders, a stalwart body, black shining eyes, and an attractive face that made every woman's head turn! But again, there was an inexplicable command and poetry in Cemal's pale gaze. There was something different in the way he bowed his shapely head; on his pale face, framed by his long, greying blond hair; on his shapely thin lips and delicate nose. Who knows what void in Seviyye's soul this solemn-looking, blue-eyed teacher had filled? And who knows what kindred connection Seviyye had found in him that was compatible with the highlife she dreamed of.

From the moment Cemal arrives until he leaves, my unruly mind is occupied with Seviyye. I think about her adventurous life in all its details. And then I feel the devoted, infinite love of a woman surrounding Cemal! An affection so strong that they look down upon the values of others and defy all the humiliation and torture in that world, every passing minute! God, what wild, passionate, unrivaled vibes must embrace this calm, middle-aged, pale-looking piano teacher? My mind involuntarily wanders after their love affair for hours. And then I find myself feeling jealous of this pianist who incites such curiosity and perhaps a little envy in others. I am now certain that the divine voice I heard on that road was Seviyye's. This voice pours all its passion and ecstasy, rapture and suffering only onto this ugly, gaunt man's soul. The treasures of love, virtue, and personality are all spread under his feet! My God, what is it about these artists that they can enchant and subdue the most powerful women, the most headstrong beauties? I wonder if women are a bit like the snakes and music is the antidote for their poison and danger.

More than anyone, Samime was against Macide studying under Cemal. She was stunned that Macide could take lessons from a man who broke apart another family. And she chastised me the most because we are allies in condemning Seviyye's wrongful actions. Macide and Numan, on the other hand, take Seviyye's side. I am guessing Samime may be a little jealous of Numan, who after all, has stayed so loyal to his young aunt for all these years. Perhaps she senses some kind of danger in their friendship. I find the young woman to be justified in this. There are such mysterious, deadly tides around this woman that even a man who denounces her may feel an irresistible attraction. Because I am aware of this possibility and because I feel that I harbor such inclinations towards her, my conscience is in turmoil, and I manifest all my anger by being against her. But I spare Cemal because I know I can only see Seviyye by his means. Yes, there is that possibility and whenever I think of it, I feel dizzy with ruinous excitement. I tell myself that if ever such an opportunity arises, I shall reject it, but then again, a voice from deep inside me says: so what, it is just a curiosity!

One morning, after being counseled by Samime in *Hisar*, I teased Numan about Seviyye on the ferry. I talked to him about how objectionable it was for a young man like him to protect such a dangerous woman and that his visits to their home could cause trouble. I went even a little further and with a firm but anxious tone, I attempted to question him on the extent and true nature of his feelings for Seviyye. I wanted to do this in as much a fatherly way as I could, but my questions had such a ludicrous eagerness about them that Numan's mischievous eyes glowed with tiny mocking flickers.

"Oh! . . . Fahir, my dear, have you gone from being a moralist to a priest taking confessions?"

"Not at all, my brother. I am only saying it to protect you, so you don't waste your youth."

"Wait, my brother, no need to rush. Soon, Seviyye will invite you and Macide to her place, and then I guess you'll need to save someone else's youth!"

"No need for mockery! You must know from our time in England that I am not the kind of man to fall in love with every pair of hazel eyes."

"That is why I am scared for you. Those who don't fall in love, fall hard, head over heels."

"I had already decided to decline if Seviyye ever invited us, but now, only to prove to you what fortitude looks like, I will accept the invitation."

Numan let out a big laugh. I blushed. Then he got serious right away and approached me: "I am sorry that you still haven't changed your mind about Seviyye. Why do you find her less respectable than your wife and my wife? She considers herself to be Cemal's wife!"

"Don't be a fool! How is that possible when she is already married to another man."

"That is why I sometimes feel furious enough to kill Uncle Talip!"

However much one analyzes Numan's fondness of Seviyye, his feelings are clearly only that of a protective and devoted sibling. Strange! Strange indeed! It is hard to imagine such feelings towards women can exist in our country!

Numan stayed over at our place that night and the next day, Macide had her piano lesson. Cemal acted friendly and brotherly towards Numan and as always, shook Numan's hand in the friendliest way possible. As for us, he gave us a cold, formal greeting. Then, he walked towards Macide, with a smile on his pale lips and his pale eyes that even I couldn't help but find charming.

"You have now advanced enough to appreciate good music. My wife and I have decided to give you a concert. Would you honor us at one o'clock tonight?"

The warmth and joyful tone in his invitation disappeared when he turned towards me:

"The gentleman is also welcome to attend."

Without giving me a chance to respond, he went to the piano and started preparing Macide's music sheets.

Seviyye must be aware of Macide's fondness of her. That's why she gets all the compliments and I only get this cold invitation! Perhaps Numan tells them everything I say. In this case, the right thing for me to do is to not accept the invitation but how . . . I can't help it; I cannot show that much fortitude. Besides, I will go out of spite; I will show my disapproval of her lifestyle with my attitude.

After the meal, Macide immediately went up to her room. I knew she was busy with her evening dress. Along with her new interest in books and music, she is into evening dresses now. Dressing up like the new women! This is the biggest of her worldly desires. At first, she found it burdensome to wake up every morning, put on her corset, dress up, and follow women's fashion every month. One can even say, she was quite heedful of looking ridiculous in this new style. That probably explains why I've often overheard her and Samime in these past two months talk for hours while inspecting fabrics and patterns. Sometimes, when I notice these new habits and watch her in these new evening dresses, I think of the old Macide in her long, simple dresses. How exquisite and beautiful I had found her the day I returned from London.

I can hear her voice from my study room now. She is taking out clothes from the wardrobe and trying to put Hikmet to sleep at the same time. "Sleep, my child, and I will buy you chocolate tomorrow."

Then she calls out to me: "What do you think I should wear, Fahir?"

Without waiting for my reply, she throws away her shoes, pulls out drawers. A sharp lavender scent reaches all the way to where I am.

"Macide, I honestly cannot stand this scent."

"I wonder if England turned you into such a rude person."

Numan bursts into laughter. I get impatient; Hikmet starts getting restless. Finally, after making us wait for a long time, Macide arrives with a lamp in her hand. Her cheeks look red. Numan grabs the kerosene lamp on the desk, "O! Macide Hanım! To tell you the truth, we can't wait to see this evening dress of yours," he says.

We both start studying her dress with a smile on our faces. Our hearts are filled with such childlike joy that we cheer, rigorously flap our hands in appreciation of her looks while Macide walks around with an anxious expression that almost makes her look funny. In her new, silk, blue dress, her white coat, and the blue ribbons rising on her black hair, Macide has a young girl's naïve but charming beauty.

After we critiqued each other's evening dresses, we hit the road like three school children, arm in arm, with Macide in the middle. Once in a while, Numan held the train of Macide's skirt, acted silly and made us laugh. We had such a good time that we almost forgot where we were going. As we neared the house behind the green bushes, Macide paused, "I don't know why but I am starting to feel uneasy about this concert," she said in a fearful tone. I immediately told her that we didn't have to go. I guess, deep inside I thought that if we didn't run away from these impure people whose lives crossed paths with our peaceful and innocent lives, dark clouds would be cast over our happiness. No matter how much I had desired to see the owner of this mesmerizing voice, I dreaded to go into the house.

"What are you, little kids? You cannot possibly come all this way and turn around," said Numan, and with that ended our doubts.

A second later, we entered Seviyye's house with our best manners. An elderly Greek woman greeted us at the door and took us to the main hall. This was a large alla turca room lit by the yellow shade of two big lamps, decorated with cute white muslin curtains, large and low futons that served the comfort of the people more than anything else. The only precious object in the room was the grand piano.

As our eyes searched for the most comfortable futon, Cemal walked in with a gentle and courteous expression. He seated Macide in a futon under the lamp and across from the piano; placed pillows behind her and a footrest under her feet as deftly as a woman. Then he sat on his piano bench and addressed me, kindly: "So, you are one of Seviyye's childhood friends. Just today, Seviyye was telling me about your squabbles as kids."

Seviyye and Cemal must have talked about me then. That means Numan did not tell Seviyye about my objection to their relationship. But before I could silence my thoughts and respond to Cemal's comment, the door opened. I heard the rustle of a dress first then Seviyye walked in. How gracefully she carried the dress, as if it were an extension of her body. She still looked like the little Seviyye I remember, just older. She had a long, white, silk muslin empire waist dress on; her curvy neck and nape were exposed through a thin line that narrowed down. Her pale blonde hair was unpretentiously divided to the side and combed to her nape with a pin. Her exposed, pale forearms and face blended in with her white dress . . . Still, it was hard to say if one would find her beautiful at first sight.

Without paying attention to any of us, she walked in Macide's direction. I was standing behind Macide so I could see everything in great detail. The yellowish gleam of the lamp washed Seviyye's pale, marble-like complexion with a sweet cream color. Then she briskly lifted her eyelids, those two pure lily petals lying behind her brown eyelashes. In that moment, I could see her dark, sweet eyes smile at Macide with a warmth and affection that conquers the soul. In those dark, deep, and somewhat pleading eyes is a woman who stands up against the world, who doesn't mind being ostracized by society. No wonder Macide wrapped her arms around Seviyye hysterically; even I felt drawn to the fiery depths of her soul after a fleeting second.

After greeting Macide, Seviyye shook Numan's hand but she only greeted me from afar so I could not look into the eyes that I was so longing for. With every passing, torturous minute, I could feel her lethal beauty in the room. Even her coldness at first sight was a trick of nature! There was such supreme, ruinous might in her low-hanging, perfectly curvy shoulders, her flawless, marble skin, the thick hair that was combed on her white nape like a wheat bunch! And those dark, dazzling eyes, full of life and warmth, shaking us all to the core with their sweet sparkle, waking us from our lifeless existence, as if we were thousand-year-old statues coming back to life. She eventually sat next to Macide and with the soft intonations of her unrivaled voice, asked after Hikmet. You could hear the unconscious longing in her voice but before she had time to talk to the rest of us, Cemal turned around on the piano bench and said: "Come on, Seviyye!"

When she heard the cue, Seviyye kindly excused herself from the conversation and walked up to Cemal; lit up the candles on the piano and prepared his music sheets. I was standing in the shadow of Macide's futon, euphorically watching Seviyye move around like a white specter. Cemal's playing resonated in the room like the sound of distant waves. Seviyye waited for her turn, resting one hand on the piano, and before too long started singing. Her pale, curved neck rose and fell so beautifully with every tone of her crystal voice. I don't know why, but watching her, my throat felt tight. Suddenly, I realized and truly decried that for the first time in my life, I was being crushed and consumed by a worldly desire that took away my will power. Only the rich, commanding, captivating melody in her divine voice soothed this poisonous desire which turned me into a sickly patient, a wretched man moaning under torture. The forlorn cry in her voice seeped deep into my soul; caressed it softly, intoxicating me and healing the insanity I felt a moment ago. I was slowly being chained by infinite, golden shackles and drifting away from my past, from the young girl in blue ribbons whom I loved so much, from Numan, and from my son who was sleeping in his crib this very moment. I was being carried away in an ocean of unimaginable, deadly delights so foreign to me, my family, and friends, and I was adrift to new shores of emotions all alone. How could something so small push you off the precipitous cliffs of passion in the course of half an hour? How could it be that the Fahir who walked into this room and the helpless Fahir suffering right this moment, under the spell of this woman's voice, a voice which embodies all human emotion, are not the same person?

In the final part of the concert, Seviyye sang Schumann's song cycle, based on poems by Heine. It was all in German, so I could not follow the songs, but it was obvious she grasped every word fully, laying bare the soul of the poet in beautiful tones, with a piercing, humbling pain. When she left the piano there wasn't a dry eye in the room. All of us, including Cemal, worshipped Seviyye's disarming might like helpless, obedient slaves. It is true that we all worship at the altar of beauty but with Seviyye, there was also this divine voice, descending from the heavens, which had the power to make anyone prostrate! That night, before we left, Seviyye honored one last song request from Macide. She walked to the piano and whispered something into Cemal's ear. At that moment, though I was looking down, I could sense the sweet flickers that I adored so much, dancing on my forehead. Alas, I kept my eyes down with a deep sense of fear and helplessness; scared and intoxicated, I dared not meet her eyes.

She started right away with the aria: "White and exquisite, like a rose . . ." How the aria described the newborn sensations that burned my soul like the scorching sun. I pictured her fifteen years ago, in her white headwear; her exceptional, small, elegant face convulsing with heartache. In that moment, a victorious, happy voice inside me violently confessed that I had loved her since I was a child.

The final key in her voice adorned our enraptured souls with bright and dazzling lights. I lifted my eyes right before our hopeless and grief-stricken souls were about to crash into a dark void, and sent her camellia-like face, the seat of her divine voice, a mad, worshipping kiss from my soul.

Back home, in our bedroom, Macide was still awake. "Haven't you fallen asleep yet, Macide?"

"That voice tugs at my heartstrings. It was so sublime, wasn't it?"

"It was not bad."

"Not bad? Fahir, nothing's good enough for you."

"Have a good night, my dear!"

Half an hour later, Macide was peacefully asleep. I, on the other hand, knowing deep inside that I would never be able to sleep again, waited for the morning light to appear at my dark window.

Futile Conflict

October 8, 1908

"White and exquisite like a rose . . ." She was right there in front of me when I opened my eyes; her dazzling body dancing among soft, white, tulle clouds; her curved neck moving like crystal waves!

I feel a terrifying joy in my heart. It's as if my entire body is tyrannized, burning, and trembling violently with intense yearnings. I am caught in a tempest when I expected it least, but I am no longer at the helm and giant currents are drifting me away from my loved ones, my home, and my principles in life, to distant shores. The pillars that have guided me in telling right from wrong in life, pillars that I believed in, are gone. I am spiraling forward in ecstasy at a dizzying speed.

I was glad when Numan left in the morning. The truth is, I want to get away from familiar eyes, especially Macide's trusting, tranquil, black eyes. I know, I should be tormented with those black eyes but all I have in my heart for her is compassion. How could it be that this woman who was so close to my soul yesterday, is no longer in my heart and mind. How little can separate two minds and two hearts from each other!

I feel an unfamiliar sense of treachery growing in me. Life's trivialities seem so foreign, so frivolous that I just smile at, even remain indifferent to, things that used to infuriate me. My biggest desire is to see Seviyye and find a way to hear her voice again. And, of course, only Macide can make that happen.

One more thing: I want to be alone and explore the new shapes and colors of my thoughts. Yes, who would have thought that I harbored such delightful, soul-caressing, coy thoughts; such suffering, weakness, and longings in my heart? I don't know this new Fahir who has a towering cascade of yearnings pouring into his heart. In that heart, there is such an eagerness to live and experience life with all its mysteries, subtleties, meanings, and desires.

October 10
I woke up feeling empty. The mad turbulence of the last two days has subsided and left its place to a silent sorrow. I now believe that it was nothing other than an intense infatuation that caused such a violent upheaval in me. And once its cause disappeared, so did the longing. But all this cautioned me against a danger lying ahead. I now under-stand that seeing Seviyye will be absolutely ruinous for me. Yes, it will be an irresistible oasis of heavenly dreams but an abyss for me and my entire family! I made up my mind. I will never see Seviyye again.

Today, my returning affection and compassion towards Macide
is strong enough to bring tears to my eyes! I woke up early this
morning and watched her sleeping next to me, peaceful like a child.
She looked rather beautiful with her tall, elegant, perfectly shaped
body; her small and dark complexion animated with the shadow plays
of her elegant eyebrows, black eyelashes, and her small, pink mouth.
And yet, I only watch her beauty like an admiring friend, study it
with the observing gaze of an artist. How I thought I loved her until
recently. Though she doesn't know the true nature of my affection
for her right now, here I am, fully aware of and feeling desolate
about how I should be loving her. And then I think about seeing
Seviyye in that room . . . even the dream of seeing her again
shudders me with fiery shivers.

Forlorn and lost, I try to gather my thoughts. I try to remember,
go back to the beginnings of my life with Macide, and map out the
anatomy of my feelings for her back then. It was four years ago. My
poor mother was in the last stages of a heart disease that ended up
taking her from us. That was the first time I felt Macide's presence
in my life. Until then she was just a shy, puny young brunette who
was brought over by my aunt to our house every bayram to kiss
my father's hand. I believe my father was particularly fond of her.
My mother, who shared all my father's feelings and interests on
every issue in life, naturally showed affection towards Macide, too,
and treated her well-though she didn't really care much for my
aunt. As for me, I don't ever recall taking a real interest in Macide.

I remember how I pulled her long, thick, tightly braided hair one day. It was meant to be a joke but she was upset and had blushed right away. So, I decided right then that she wasn't good enough to be a playmate for me, and I never again bothered with her. Things changed with my father's death. In those days, whenever I came back from school, I would find Macide in the house. How she used to attend to my mother in her serious and somber way. She would light her cigarettes, and sometimes engage in deep conversations. I never quite understood why my mother, who was always joyful and full of life, would be interested in Macide's company. I always thought it was out of respect for my father's memory.

One day, as Macide was leaving the room, my mother pointed to Macide, and said: "I wish I had an earnest daughter-in-law like her, then I would die a happy mother, knowing that I leave you in the hands of a woman who would love you faithfully, with the dedication of a mother and friend."

That day, I dropped the subject right away. It drove me crazy to even think about the death of my mother. But I now see that it was my mother's biggest wish to see Macide and me get married.

Days went by. On the day I returned home with my diploma, I found my mother bedridden. In the dark days that followed, I got used to the presence of a graceful and dignified woman in the house, attending to my sick mother like an affectionate, old nurse. It was as if all of a sudden, I had started to enjoy watching the shadows of the silky hair on her nape. In time, I learned to respect the dignified calmness on her young face. My mother's pleas for our marriage no longer upset me. Finally, as we stood in front of my mother's death bed, our hands united for a lifetime, delighted to enter into what we dreamt would be a calm, peaceful life.

We got married two months after my mother's death. We wanted to honor the dearly departed's wish and also take consolation in each other's arms as we grieved for this noble woman. How bereft we were of the lovesickness that is overtaking my soul now.

I remember being overcome by a strange excitement that day when I saw Macide in her white bridal veil, sitting in the middle of that sofa, with the calmness and patience of an old woman. She hadn't even blushed when I lifted her veil. There was such virginal, innocent trust, and affection in her black eyes that right away I could imagine a life of perfect harmony in front of me. But alas! Isn't this woman, a wife of four years and a mother, isn't she going to wake up one day from this sweet dream and ask for more than her husband's distant and silent friendship, his solicitous affection? Isn't she going to regret it when she realizes that the man to whom she relinquished all the treasures of her youth didn't let her live life to the fullest, with all its tempests and passions?

Now I understand that no matter how painful and destructive it may be, it would be a loss, in fact it would be humanity's biggest loss, to die without being in touch with that divine might, being in harmony with nature, without hearing those most tempestuous words that turn your world upside down, without trembling, without weeping. But alas, how many eyes had lost their glimmer, waiting for that elusive, divine feeling, and how many hearts had stopped, suffering, waiting for it? I remember one of my friends, a rather stern, dignified, and middle-aged family man once telling me, "In this life, I had whatever it takes to make man happy, but I never got rid of the strange feeling that something was missing. I know that what visits even the hearts of the most ill-fated, the most wretched has never visited mine and I cannot help but feel as if there is a vast untouched, empty void in my heart."

I don't know why but listening to him that day, I, too, had felt I was forever waiting for something to arrive, and shivered at the possibility of it never arriving.

For the last two days, my heart has rejoiced with the arrival of expected news. Now I laugh at my efforts to run away from her, to uproot her from my heart, and replace it with this unpleasant sorrow. How horrible a thing human frailty is! It can upend everything: marriages and sometimes even governments established by the will of millions, and therefore an entire country!

I walked around with Macide all day today. I even came in between her and her books. I want to penetrate into her heart, take refuge in her tranquil soul and forget this strange sorrow. But she is not herself

today. She doesn't seem to notice the strangeness in me. She is
unusually joyful. Her laughter fills the house. In her black eyes dwells
a surprise she is trying to hide and dying to reveal at the same time.

After dinner, she suddenly came near me in her charshaf and pulled
me by the arm, smiling at me. She said she was going to *Hisar* and was
encouraging me to get ready. So, I got up and started getting ready.

October 11

Last night, I noticed Macide and Samime talking in whispers in a far
corner. Once in a while they would whisper something in Numan's
ear, but whenever I walked in, they stopped talking. I knew they were
preparing a surprise, but I didn't have the strength to be curious.
Instead, I stayed on the balcony and watched the dark waters in the
sea beat the rocks with threatening, resentful strokes.

Later that night, as I was drifting off in bed, Macide, sounding a bit
upset with my lack of interest in the whole thing, said: "I wish you
knew what a victory this is for me!"

"What victory? Are you dreaming?"

"I will bring Samime and Seviyye together. Don't you see that I have
been planning things for the last couple of days? On Monday, all of
us will take an oxcart ride to *Kayışdağı*, and ride back in moonlight.
Think of Seviyye's voice on that road! Fahir, why aren't you saying
anything?"

How could I have answered her when I couldn't even breathe? My heart was beating with such pain, racing with such force! Squeezing Macide's arm as tightly as I could, I said in a low voice: "I will not join you. Besides why do you make it your business to make peace between people?"

How I rioted against this endeavor that would ruin both of us. But, poor child, how could she have known the tempest brewing around her? At first, she got angry that her plans weren't approved and that I was ruining her one and only wish, then she said in despair, with tears in her eyes: "What will I do now after I have already planned everything? How will I look at people's faces?"

When she realized I wasn't answering her, she let out a sigh and closed her eyes. At that moment, I felt profoundly sorry for this child and for myself. The more I tried to listen to my conscience and do the right thing the more obstacles I seemed to face. But that wasn't all; I had lost my mind with a terrifying joy that obliterated everything. The thought of being in the same place, the same carriage as Seviyye; to weep listening to her voice, to be intoxicated with her smallest gesture! I was thinking about her all the time. Until Monday, my nights would be white and bright with her light.

I bent over to Macide, and said quietly: "Forgive me, my dear. I didn't mean to be ungrateful. I'll go anywhere you want me to go."

Oh, how hypocritical and wretched people can be!

October 13

The day that I have been waiting for so anxiously has come and gone by. I am left heartbroken; for all that my heart was secretly longing for passed right by me without the faintest touch. That morning, I was feeling rather weary and melancholic. It felt strange that the day I had been longing for could start like any other day. All morning, Macide and Samime chatted about their evening dresses, like two chirping birds. Numan was ready before everyone else. He was all dressed up, chic, looking refreshed, walking around in a good mood. My aunt was busy carefully placing the dolma and halva in the baskets. The oxcart at the end of the street looked charming with its white canopy, red sheets, and soft pillows. There was such commotion in the house, even on the street.

Little Hikmet and I were dressing up by ourselves. I could read in his big, blue eyes, in his solemn gaze, the curiosity towards the father who has only recently entered his life. He was trying to cozy up to me little by little. But I am so absentminded and weary that I cannot pay much attention to him. Finally, after a little rush, we hear the "Let's leave" command. I see Macide and Samime dressed in carefully prepared evening dresses, their hair decorated with quite a few ribbons. I have to say, Macide looked rather beautiful in her blue coat. Samime looked pleasing and elegant in her white yeldirme; Numan was cheerful, little Hikmet, shy. My silence bored everyone a little. I told them I had a headache and asked kindly that they not mind me tonight.

The oxcart stopped at the house behind the green leaves. As soon as we arrived, Macide anxiously started up a conversation between Samime and Seviyye. I greeted Cemal but deep inside, I was bewildered by every awaiting minute when I would see Seviyye. So, it is true what they say, that there are times when happiness is insufferable. I had absolutely no courage to meet Seviyye's eyes, for I feel if she ever reveals her dark flickers to me, she will see my love for her. My mind wanders off and I think of Seviyye and I being free, unattached, but no, even then I could not be close to her, let alone marry her. If those white hands would accidentally touch my face, my bursting veins would erupt and kill me right there.

Turkish Carriage, "İstanbul Yadigarı, Souvenir de Constantinople, Voiture Turque" Postcard, 001178. Courtesy of Atatürk Library Archives, Istanbul.

I was rather quiet and melancholic on the way to *Kayışdağı*. When she handed me the food plate at the table, Seviyye's white eyelids moved up inquisitively. At that moment, I was subjected to the gaze I feared so much. I spent the rest of the day trying to recover from this shock.

That evening, on the carriage, as we were heading back, they asked her to sing, and an alla turca song, of all things! She started right away. The monotonous, tragic laments of a lover's sighs and complaints echoed on the purple mountains that turned from white to dark in the heavy-eyed night. Resting my head on the carriage post, I felt this sublime voice drowning my heart in tears and the tears streaming down my cheeks. How a person's tragic longings, torturous deprivations can transform into sweet tears. I now see with absolute certainty that I am hopelessly in love with Seviyye. This is such a powerful realization that I know all fights and resistance will be in vain.

The big moment I had unknowingly waited for all my life had finally arrived when I was least ready for it. But when it did, how tragically it made me throw the soil of oblivion on my plans, my wishes; over all those I loved dearly. Besides, I understand now that I love Seviyye neither for her beauty nor her voice. I had seen more beautiful, eminent, and glamorous women than Seviyye. And it wasn't that I loved her because she felt and thought like me. It was the cruelest trick of Fate that had made me worship the mysterious and radiant woman hiding under those lily eyelids. Now I know, there are no whys and hows in matters of the heart.

I ask myself, but what could be the harm in this? Nobody would ever know about my feelings for her. My soul would expand to cover the entire universe with all the pain and torture in this realm; the joy and ecstasy of all the stars and yet, I would still be the simple Fahir that everyone knew.

 Seviyye might have resented me today because I acted a little distant towards her. I don't know why but when she noticed the tears streaming down my face under the weight of her lovesick voice, her eyes passed mine with a big melancholic smile and caressed the most secret corners of my soul. When we were leaving, I felt her extending her white hand to me in the dark but, no, I could not summon the strength to take that hand. I respectfully bowed in front of her, and we left. On the way back, Numan started first: "To be honest, Fahir, tonight, you were as rude as a mountain bear."

Macide interrupted: "It is because he has a headache. Poor Fahir, he had to put up with all this for my sake."

Then she immediately grabbed my arm in the dark. Her affectionate little hand caressed my forehead. Macide's peaceful presence always felt so soothing, and I knew I had never wanted to depart from the decent, peaceful life I had with her. In this moment, too, it was in her friendly bosom that I could take refuge. Yes, if Macide weren't in my life, this new fire would no doubt transform me into a poor Majnun. That night, I lay in bed with her hand in mine, my eyes wide open, until the next morning. Macide was getting quite worried.

"You are burning up, Fahir. Should I get a doctor?"

"No, no. I am fine."

This is how my days go by, meaningless and full of suffering. I have latched on to Macide like a son does to his mother. The only days I feel alive are those when we visit Cemal's house!

October 23

These days, everyone stares at me strangely. They say my nerves are weak and ailed. Numan visits frequently. Macide looks sad and keeps her watchful eyes on me, always.

I, on the other hand, I only desire to be alone, always alone. Despite the cool autumn weather, I walk the hills of Çamlıca night and day. I no longer sleep. In the fields lit up by her image, every now and then I feel terrified of my own heart, my own vulnerability. Yes, I am turning into a miserable, sick man. Oh God, what would happen if the course of our lives were different? Nothing, I suppose? I would melt away in the flames of this ruinous madness. But she, she would not know a thing!

November 14

For the last couple of days, I've felt as if I am entering a new phase. Following the quiet and melancholic days come episodes of uncontrolled laughter and cheerful, loud conversations. Everyone is surprised at the awakening of my mind, and how unusually affable and outgoing I am. I laugh, I talk; I am always in search of someone to converse with.

We mostly gather at Cemal's house. My aunt has left for Istanbul. We used Macide's music lessons as an excuse to spend the winter here. Numan and Samime visit us every week. We enjoy long and delightful musical performances in Cemal's living room. Cemal seems to have gotten a few more students and the social shunning of Seviyye seems to be waning. Their friends are gradually starting to talk to them again. The sequestered life Seviyye has been living for a long time secures her a bit more trust, and people start to think that Talip Bey was unfair. I am guessing that Seviyye is quite happy with this situation. Lately, the heaviness on her eyelids and the melancholy in her manners have faded away. Her eyes, those two rare flowers, smile sweetly and give her pale face an exceptional grace. A fresh new vitality appears in her body.

My mind and soul are so whipped and excited by Seviyye's gaze that I turn into the center of attraction in this little flat. Women listen to my words with a provocative look on their faces; when we get together, Numan and Cemal find a way to make me talk. The nights are lively and joyful until I crawl into bed. Then despair presses on my shoulders like a nightmare; dark and woeful thoughts torture me until dawn. In these terrible moments, poor Macide tries to soothe me with the affection of a mother. Thankfully, she does not suspect anything. If I were to face the questions of a jealous woman while my soul is pierced with thorns, I would no doubt end my life.

I feel like a lifeless toy in the hands of ruinous desires, and with every passing minute I am withering with the yearning to see her eyes. I live for the moments when I will look into her eyes again. Her eyelids, as soft and delicate as lilies, will quickly lift up and I will see those dark flickers, those two magnificent passages to her soul. You see, I live waiting for that deadly moment.

One evening, not long ago, I was being overly talkative. I must have grabbed Seviyye's attention because she stared at me for a long time. I was so enchanted and afflicted by the allure of those sweet eyes that in the middle of my conversation, I suddenly collapsed. Everyone gathered around me.

"Recently, he has been feeble and frail like this. It is because of all those sleepless nights," Macide said.

I got up, apologizing to everyone. I was so mortified at the thought of Seviyye coming by and asking after me that I stormed out. Numan tried to give me a hand. Desperate and perplexed, Macide and Samime followed my every move. As soon as we arrived home, I buried my head in Macide's skirt and sobbed for a long time.

November 15

Today, Macide had her piano lesson. Seviyye had come along with Cemal to check up on me.

"Last night you ran away without giving me a chance to ask how you were feeling," Seviyye said, gently.

My old melancholic and quiet mood is back. I am so feverish and lethargic that even Seviyye's very existence couldn't wipe away the dark and thick sorrow covering my soul. After observing Macide's lesson for a while, Seviyye went next door to play with Hikmet.

"Fahir, go inside" Macide said from the piano bench "Don't leave Seviyye Hanım by herself."

I followed Seviyye like a beat-up kid. Alas, the very first time we could finally be alone was not a moment of joy but of torment.

When she heard me walk in, she stopped playing with the child and sat on the futon. She clasped her hands on her knees nervously. I could sense that she wanted to say something to me, but I was terrified to lift up my eyes. I leaned on the window, trying hard to stop my hands from shaking.

She started to talk in an affectionate tone:

"Aren't you going to sit down, Fahir Bey? Please go ahead, yes, sit on the armchair. I see that your condition hasn't improved much since last night. We are childhood friends," she said gently, "and that is why

I have the right to know what is going on with you. I see that you have been unwell for a while now. Macide Hanım told me that it is your nerves. Have you seen a doctor?"

"Macide and I are visiting all the neurologists in Istanbul. But I do it only to make her happy; otherwise, I don't really think I need a doctor."

Seviyye, unsure of her next step, remained silent for a few minutes. Then she started to talk resolutely, determined to do something about it: "I, too, was suffering from a sickness just like yours."

"Recently?"

"No. Before I made the decision to leave Talip Bey."

Hearing this, my heart almost jumped out of my chest. So, Seviyye knows about my illness. My head was spinning. Though she understands what I am going through, she acts rather indifferently and with a sisterly affection towards me.

"I knew right away when I saw your troubles and I was worried about you like a sister. One is condemned to suffer through such agony alone though, right?"

I remained silent. I could no longer respond.

"Anyway, in my case, there was a solution. So, I could in the end cure my nervous disease."

"How did you do it?" I asked her courageously.

"By shaping up my life the way I wanted to, but I guess this is not really possible for you, right?"

"I don't know."

"What do you mean you don't know? she said, looking at Hikmet playing on the floor, "I didn't have any sacred ties. I could morally justify my breakup with Talip Bey. And, Cemal wasn't married."

Oh, God! This woman was going to be the end of me. What else would she say, how much more suffering could she inflict upon me?

"In your case, it is impossible. One cannot sacrifice Numan and Macide for one's personal happiness."

At that moment, it all dawned on me in a flash of lightning. So, she thinks I am in love with Samime. This is how she interpreted my rather close and brotherly friendship with Samime. Whatever it was, I was madly joyous that she was concerned about me, and that her concern led to these private moments. I almost wanted to confirm her suspicions; talk to her privately about my love. Ah, to be able to say it all to this woman who has cruelly stolen my nights from me, tell it all as if telling it to a third person . . . This was such ruinous desire that I could barely stop myself from resting my head on her feet and pouring out the poison in my heart with my tears. Instead, I said with a faint, choked voice: "Thank you. You understand me well. But this is such madness that it'll either drag me to death or murder. If I have one consolation, it's that she will never know about my suffering."

"How? You don't think she noticed? If a woman awakens such interest in a man, she will naturally know."

"And sometimes she may not."

Seviyye regarded me with suspicion, but her face regained its old clarity right away.

"I will give you some advice now. Would you indulge me?"

"Without a doubt!"

"Travel."

"Never! It would kill me to be away from her."

"Then please talk to a friend about your situation. Would it not drive you mad to be in this hopeless tragedy and also to have to hide it?"

"Would you allow me to visit you from time to time and talk to you about my suffering?"

"I would like to be honest with you, as an old friend should. The delicate situation I am in compels me to tread even more carefully and act even more conservatively. Besides, despite his calm looks, Cemal is an incredibly jealous man. But, if there are coincidences like this, I will listen to you."

"Can't I write to you?"

"That, my dear, is all the more impossible because I share all my letters with Cemal. There are no secrets between us. If there is no harm in him seeing your letters, then do it."

"Never!"

Her last sentence had reopened my wound. I shivered with an incredible desire to destroy, to kill this pale-faced teacher who was playing Czerny etudes to Macide on the piano with forte, staccato beats next door.

November 23

I am back at wandering around with my old ill-tempered, melancholic self. Until recently, my soul languished with a hopeless desire to be happy but now I am going mad with a rage and hatred that frightens me. With every passing day, this feeling of rage transforms into a desire to take revenge. I now shiver as much when I see Cemal as I do Seviyye, but for other reasons! If this man didn't exist, perhaps Seviyye would have loved me. Then . . . then we would run away from it all and go wherever life took us!

But what about Macide and Hikmet?

I let out a shriek of laughter that startled Macide. Yes, I had startled myself, too with what I saw inside my soul. After starting a bloody battle for my ideals, I was ready to abandon child, wife, morals, everything and run away. So, this is I, a wretched man; I, who thought he had a role in the struggles of his country; I, who had promised to carry out the onerous mission of the new faction in his own being, ready to abandon everything and run away like a coward, all for a woman. I could not live without her, and I lacked the courage to die for her. Fate had made me sacrifice my ideals, my youth, and more . . . Oh, God. I am tormented by the thought of my weakness staining the honor of the reformers, humiliating those who are going to save the country. . . . Could there be any bigger betrayal than this? A betrayal of the homeland, child, wife, and even a betrayal of the future! You poor, poor young people! Will your fight to stay strong, to advance, be wrecked, toppled down with the hand of a woman? Are all fights against love this futile?

December 3

For the last ten days, I find myself to be a little bit stronger. But I still don't trust myself much. I now understand that the only remedy left for me is to travel. I am making my plans. First, I will go and live by myself for five or six months. If I don't heal by then, I will call for Macide and bury my sorrows under a different canopy, into the depths of other horizons. No doubt that running away is the most heroic thing to do in this case. But I wonder if even that will remain a futile attempt? Will I return in a month or two, more violently passionate and weaker than before? My mind is constantly preoccupied with *Anthony and Cleopatra*. I am always thinking about that epic hero abandoning the battlefield and his military honor and running after Cleopatra like a frightened kid. What a glorious name he left behind in the battlefield, what valiant character, what devoted, loyal brothers in arms. But was I not like him? I was weak and feeble enough to abandon all my principles, my wife, child, life, morals, everything, with just a sign from her. In these moments, I am repulsed with myself and then an intense pity takes over. In the end, I think that I am the most miserable of them all.

December 4

After a terrible night, I went to Istanbul to see a doctor. I told him that I was going mad and no matter how much I tried, I felt like I was nearing the abyss. I wanted to run away, from myself, from everything around me. The doctor supported my travel plans. In fact, he presented it to me as an absolute necessity. He advised me especially to be in places where I could socialize. "It is the season for Monte Carlo, and a little gambling feat wouldn't be such a bad thing for you" he said.

My mind was busy with travel plans until the evening. I could see new desires, new hopes on the horizon. For the first time in two months, I was going back home in a good mood. Macide, whose eyes meticulously watched every little change in me was as happy as a little child when she saw me like this. At night, I had a long talk with her about the travel plans I made under the supervision of my doctor. She listened to me with a sad but serious expression. Her little hands were convulsing nervously around my hands. She was acknowledging the necessity of the trip and wasn't opposed to it. But she was also doing her best to hide the knots of sorrow forming in her throat. Tonight, it was my turn to console and soothe her. From here on, we were two ill-fated souls. I loved this affectionate woman who never let go of my hand, with reverence and sincerity, above all other love. We lay in each other's arms with such devotion, devoid of all materiality; with our souls knit so close, that I feared this to be a permanent goodbye. Right before dawn, I heard Macide talking in her sleep as if she could read my melancholic thoughts: "You will never come back, right?"

December 7

As I was returning from *Uzun Yol* that afternoon, Numan appeared
out of nowhere.

"Why didn't you tell me that you were departing tomorrow? I just left
your house. Macide told me about your travel plans. But tell me, is it
true that you haven't decided on a destination yet?"

"I intend to take the Orient Express to Paris!"

"Come on, admit that your illness is an excuse to go to Europe!"

"Please, enough with the idle talk. I am shivering; I'll go back home."

"I was just going to Seviyye. Would you like to come along?"

"No!" I said firmly.

And yet, here I was, going back home, regretting what I had just
said. I just couldn't apprehend how I could willingly turn down my
last chance to see her. At dinner time, as each of us were woefully
contemplative but for different reasons. A few minutes later, the
servant delivered a letter from Numan:

Fahir and Macide,

I mentioned Fahir's travel plans to Seviyye. While everyone was sad to hear about it, they were also happy for his health. Their initial plan was to come to your place tonight but Cemal's sisters are visiting from Hungary, so they are inviting you over instead. One of the sisters plays the violin. There is a musical feast tonight!

As soon as I saw the mademoiselles I regretted being married. Having said that, this means, in Samime's absence, there is a flirt feast for me tonight! Please don't wait for me at dinnertime. And come here as quickly as possible.

Numan

Note: Fahir, the evening dresses are unbelievable. Tell Macide to put on her most fetching dress.

N.

Macide seemed a little upset with this invitation. I could see how she wanted to spend our last night together. But I could not possibly miss this final chance to see Seviyye. It wasn't easy but I eventually persuaded her to attend. The hope of seeing Seviyye in an hour had already made me forget about the trip, everything, even the food on the table.

Despite Numan's annoying reminders, Macide dressed up only when
I obliged her to do so. She wasn't in the mood. But, in the end as
soon as she started getting ready, she was overtaken by a sense of
rivalry and quickly lost herself in her preparations for the night. In
the meantime, I had to walk Hikmet around for a good hour before
he finally fell asleep. After I put him to sleep, Macide asked me to her
room to show me her evening dress.

As soon as I saw her, I was astounded by the immense role the
environment could have on a woman's morality. When you think
about it, the simple and shy Macide that I met when I returned from
London was very different from the one standing in front of the
mirror, victoriously proud of her fresh, youthful looks. Back then she
was against seeing Numan, even with her headscarf on, though she'd
known him since childhood and though he was like a brother to me.
And now, she was going to Cemal's, virtually a stranger's house in a
tight dress, nearly half-naked.

She was wearing a tulle, cream-colored, long imperial dress. Her
neckline descended beautifully. Soft, tiny golden pleats that caressed
her sweet, cream-colored skin sparkled around her décolleté. Her
arms were covered with the same cream-colored tulle. There was
a belt made of the same golden pleat that started from under her
arms and folded on her breast. This long tulle with its fine creases,
intimated the elegance and youth of the body under it without
revealing too much. Her evenly separated black hair cast vibrant

shadows on the tiny, dark face and her fine features. The two
golden roses on the sides of her hair completed this tableau.
With a heartfelt, involuntary cheer, I said: "You are more beautiful
than Seviyye!"

At that moment, victory and suspicion cast their shadow on Macide's
face. The way I compared her to Seviyye had perplexed her. "So, you
find Seviyye beautiful then?" she asked.

"I used to find her pretty but now that I see a beauty above of all
beauties in front of me, I changed my mind."

"Come on, you hypocrite!" she said, smiling at me:

We had averted the storm. I helped Macide with her heavy coat. Arm
in arm, we left home. Numan greeted us light-heartedly at Cemal's
door. As soon as the doors of the main hall opened, he whispered into
Macide's ear, "The one on the right is the queen of my heart," pointing
at two rather elderly mademoiselles wearing glasses and bonnets.
Macide was trying hard not to laugh.

As soon as he noticed us, Cemal stopped speaking Hungarian with
his sisters and greeted us in French. Because the mademoiselles
didn't know any Turkish, we had to speak French, too. It was poor
Macide who was having a difficult time. She could speak and
understand a little English but no French. But there was a solution
for that, too. It so happened that the mademoiselles knew some

English, and Cemal seemed to know enough to get by as well. Numan, Seviyye and I, had already grown up with English.

Numan kept on paying poetic compliments to Mademoiselle Line while he was talking to me in Turkish on the side: "You have to see Seviyye tonight. She is half naked . . . I guess those who change their lives, even though it may be the right thing to do, lose a bit of their moral integrity and purity in the end."

"Watch your words; Cemal will hear you."

"Look, she is coming."

I looked at her and saw it for myself. The blood gushed to my cheeks, and I shivered with wicked, bestial desires.

It looked as if Seviyye had dressed up for a specific purpose tonight. I wondered if she was half naked because she knew we were coming, or was this simply a coincidence? Yes, this woman embodies the same fruitfulness of life, and abundance of sensuality as Messalina and Cleopatra, and I think that Nature has especially sent her to turn the world upside down. A magnificent, ruinous might flows through her entire body. She is in such stark contrast with Macide's beautiful, noble, virgin-like figure, her graceful face. Even the small décolleté that I considered too much is nothing but an innocent tableau of chastity compared to the breathtaking shoulders of Seviyye.

A soft, champagne-colored crêpe de Chin covered her entire body
and fell to her feet. Her arms and shoulders were entirely naked. Only
two pieces of champagne-colored silk fluttered on her shoulders,
like butterflies. No trimming spoiled the tight ruffles on her dress. Her
hair was combed on her neck. If hues of red light did not flicker on
the ends of her blonde hair, her hair too would join her pale skin, and
if it wasn't for the light blonde hair on her nape, one could think she
is an immaculate marble statue. But there is a hellish beauty in this
perfect body. The broad shoulders, thin waist, and curvy hips could
ruin you in flames.

When she greeted me, there was a friendly sparkle in her eyes that
seemed to approve of my decision to travel. Tonight, I find her so
enchanting, so attractive, and cheerful that my desire to travel
melts away. I believe the Romans' pomp of pleasures has left its
pale echoes on her lily-like body tonight and I feel lightheaded with
pleasures akin to the ancient tribe which lived intoxicated with
flowers, grandeur, and beauty. Tonight, I made up my mind. I will
most certainly leave for Egypt tomorrow. I will live the two-thousand-
year-old heartache all over again. I will sit under the dream-like palm
trees that throw their shade on the Nile's green, poisonous waters
and listen to the memories of Cleopatra from the white water lilies.
Desolate and conquered by the dream of this woman whose eyes
are made of fire and her lips of poison, I will be destined to a lifetime
of feverish torment.

Time flies away tonight, and I cannot seem to fully grasp what's going on around me. Seviyye recites Khayyam's *Rubaiyat* in English in her mellifluous voice. As this melancholic, golden voice sings of ancient lines about the end of the spring, withering roses, beautiful bodies that turn into dust, I feel that the fever that has arrested me for the last few months is now scorching my soul. I feel something fluttering inside me, burning up my temples and wrists, making me lose myself.

"Ah, moon of my delight, who know'st no wane!"

Yes, the unwaning moon of delight and the source of torture! Since I am running away from you, the last drop of your poison and flames don't matter that much, right?

Seviyye asked Macide in her stoic, golden voice: "Where is Fahir Bey going for his travels?"

At that moment, that ill-fated, great general's lines that reveal his weakness and tragic fall poured out of my mouth, as if I was mumbling to myself.

"Oh, whither hast thou led me, Egypt?"

I could read the decree on my shame in her eyes . . .

As if she knew the whole tragedy by heart, Seviyye started reciting the lines in her perfect English, breathing life into the character with her delicious, playful tone:

"O my lord, my lord,
Forgive my fearful sails! I little thought
You would have followed"

At that moment, unable to restrain my soul from speaking through my eyes, I let the words spill from my lips:

"Egypt, thou knew'st too well
My heart was to thy rudder tied by th' strings,
And thou shouldst tow me after. O'er my spirit
Thy full supremacy thou knew'st, and that
Thy beck might from the bidding of the gods
Command me."

This seemingly joke-like exchange brought clouds to Cemal's face, and a bitter gaze to Macide's innocent eyes. Numan was taken aback. "I can recite all the lines of the *Tragedy of Antony and Cleopatra* from memory," Seviyye said, without losing her calmness.

But the mood in the room had changed irreversibly. The rest of the evening was quite formal. I had now lost all my willpower, and drifted from this miserable realm, with a new and infinite kind of ecstasy. I was blacking out. The only light I could see was the movement of her magnificent shoulders. The sweet notes dancing on her crystal throat elated us in their supreme purity. No doubt that her brutally beautiful and round breasts were the golden chalice gods used on Mt. Olympus. What wouldn't I give to drink the fire of life from those dark eyes covered with lily-eyelids? I would gladly bury honor and life but also the entire universe, the stars, and the sun in complete darkness for that.

Macide and Numan were outside already. I was by the door, putting on my shoes. I felt the rustling of silk behind me. The lights in the hallway were all of a sudden out. As I was leaning on the door, waiting, her white, kind hand squeezed mine, and in a low voice, she said: "Please forgive me. I understand it all now."

Shivering like a sick child between Macide and Numan, I headed home. Macide walked in a deep, stubborn silence. Numan was holding my hand sympathetically. But the real fever started when I arrived home. The thumping at my temples intensified. It was as if my entire life cascaded to my temples, about to burst out of my veins. I was burning with a terrible fever and could no longer see the objects around me. All I saw in front of my eyes was a pale face and a curvy body just like the chalice of the Olympian gods, amidst the white mist, glowing in golden lights, and I heard a sweet voice lamenting in golden sound waves above me. I was weeping, laughing, singing, begging, but always following that white vision.

"Beautiful and white like a rose . . ."

The more I reached out for her, the further she disappeared in the distance. Finally, I cried out "Seviyye! Seviyye!" to this vision, the absolute owner of my soul.

At that moment, I felt the presence of a poor, abandoned, heart-broken young woman weeping on the armchair, and saw the face of a loyal friend, who looked like Numan, trying to put me to bed.

December 8

This morning, I woke up with the doctor's face in front of me, and Numan standing next to my bed. They both look at me rather differently today. Macide was nowhere to be seen. I couldn't summon the courage to ask about Macide. My fragmented memory tells me that she has learned about everything.

"You had quite a nervous breakdown last night, but it shouldn't keep you from starting your travels today. In fact, this trip could even prove beneficial for you," said the doctor, trying to look cheerful.

"I am coming with you," Numan added, smiling at me.

Now I know. They look at me as if I have gone mad after my nervous breakdown last night. And they don't dare leave me alone because they don't trust me. But then, I don't have the energy to protest any of this. All my youth's constraint and repressions exploded last night. Now, like a helpless and obedient child, I give them control over my life.

I dressed up, grabbed my already packed bags and calmly followed Numan to the carriage in front of the door. I had no courage to request seeing Hikmet and Macide. As I was passing by my aunt's door, I heard the sobs of the woman whose little heart I heard break last night and my aunt's harsh words to her, "This is what Westernization will get you!"

Numan went up to the telegram house in *Üsküdar Harbor* and sent Samime a rather long telegram. Then he turned to me and said: "I know you have decided to leave with the Orient Express, but unlike you I don't have a passport to take the train. Wouldn't it be better if we took the Osmaniye Ferry of the Khedivial Company, which is leaving the harbor today, and spend this miserable winter in a warm place like Egypt, together?"

"Yes, but the doctor recommended Monte Carlo."

"Don't worry about that. I talked to the doctor last night. We made this plan together."

"If that's the case, why do you even ask me? Take me wherever you like."

I was going through a nervous fit that made me especially impatient with small talk. I didn't have the will to do anything. I would go wherever they wanted to drag me. I didn't care.

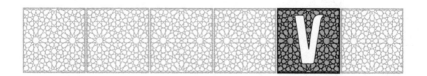

Heartache

December 10

For the last two days, I have been feeling rather melancholic and lethargic, and I don't feel like leaving the cabin. I hardly ever speak to Numan. He, on the other hand, follows me everywhere with his anxious, woeful eyes.

Today, I feel like there is enough life in me to feel ashamed of myself. I obsessively revisit the last incident and how it struck like lightning. I am trying to determine the extent of my responsibility and guilt in all of this. But alas, I feel almost certain that if I were to relive the last few days, I would act exactly the same way! Ah, human frailty; so, we are nothing more than puppets in the hands of our hearts. A well-lived life, long-standing spiritual abstinence, and life-long principles can easily be wrecked for a woman's spellbinding eyes. I wonder if I was just born weak and everyone else is made of stronger material? But again, I hadn't done anything to betray my principles or my wife, had I? I was tormented by such agonizing longings and yearnings to the point of being mentally and physically ailed but still,

I had not uttered a word to Seviyye. Would I be guilty if I told Macide the suffering, the wretchedness in my soul, the temporary insanity, the fever that drags my being into oblivion? If I think of it this way, my thoughts flow in all directions, and I manage to collect enough evidence to conclude that I am not the guilty one but a victim. How one can fabricate so much witty evidence to justify his desires! Thankfully, this infirmity in me doesn't last very long. Even if I were innocent until now, I would no doubt be guilty from now on if I don't try to leave behind this madness. Poor Macide! How she sobbed with the innocence of a heartbroken child. My biggest crime towards her would be to pretend like I am healed when in fact, I am not. How much it betrayed her trust to see me weak and helpless after I assured her for years that I had a moral compass. She will no longer believe me, that's for sure. Does she at least understand that my infidelity is only in my heart and mind, and that I am wrestling with insanity and even death to stop it from materializing into anything?

Today, my willpower, weakened by sudden decisions at times, is strained. My inner voice tells me "Even if you cannot forget about your love, can't you at least bury it so deep that you would not ever see it?" Yes, until my last breath, my arms will remain open to Seviyye, with a dark yearning. But can't I be strong enough to keep this a secret for eternity? The only way this could happen is if I lived among crowds, in foreign lands, and engaged in the lives of others. I started putting that to a test today on the ship. For the first time, I went downstairs to eat at the table, tried to observe people and find joy in others' ideas and emotions. Numan must have sensed my new decision, for he looked cheerful. Even though we both know what's going on, we do not talk about the incident. I know he will write to Macide everything about me. Poor little Macide! Maybe her little heart will be relieved to hear that I am gaining some strength and am healing.

At the table, sitting across from me, are two beautiful Russian mademoiselles and, I believe, an Austrian. She is not all that pretty, but there is such deep sorrow on her melancholic face and heavy eyelids. What could possibly be tormenting such a young girl? Her face soothes me. Numan on the other hand, is interested in the Russian mademoiselles. An overweight businessman is traveling to Egypt with a pale-faced young boy. He must be his son. You see a profound bitterness towards life in the eyes of the boy. It must be because of his illness. I can almost see him watch the rosy cheeks of the Russian mademoiselles with spite and envy.

I examine everyone at the table, one by one. Then, with a sudden sense of rebellion, I am taken over by a desire to run away. Ah, if only they knew how that woman with lips of fire and eyes of poison lures me into the depths of the calm waters with irresistible melodies!

December 11
Two rather old British women boarded the boat in Athens. One of them happened to sit next to me at the table. I noticed from her accent that she is American. Her small face is covered with wrinkles. She has such meaningful, smart, sweet eyes behind her

big glasses! Her favorite thing is to talk about philosophy. I sense that she and I will be good friends in no time. We spend the entire day together. Poor old woman, because she cannot resolve life's riddles with experiences, she wants to classify the world according to dry hypotheses and theories!

December 12

Miss Hopkins and I have truly become inseparable friends. Engaging in intellectual debates with this smart woman on philosophical and scientific questions keeps me busy during the day. Exhausted after a good debate, we talk about our favorite poets. Whichever name I utter in our conversations, she can find a book by that poet in her chest. Yesterday, for quite some time, she read to me from Dante in English translation. But when it came to Paolo and Francesca, in fear of an approaching storm in my heart, I said: "Please, don't read that."

She nodded with the kindness of noble souls. There was such profound compassion and shelter in her eyes that I teared up, but afraid of revealing my tears, I rushed to the deck, saying I needed some fresh air. When I came back inside and sat next to her, she started to talk about Plato's *Republic* as if nothing had happened.

December 13

Early this morning, we arrived in Alexandria. If there is one strange thing about friendship on boats, it is that there are no sad goodbyes. Miss Hopkins and I were cheerful as we bid farewell to each other.

Numan said with a mischievous wink: "To be honest, this friendship seems stronger than the rest. If I were to write to Macide about this, it would extinguish the flames of the Seviyye affair."

But the minute her name left his lips, Numan regretted uttering the name that put us on this boat in the first place.

"Ah, Fahir. I am mostly to blame for your misfortune. You were living happily and peacefully and I dragged that woman into your life."

Squeezing the hands of this loyal friend, I said: "No, Numan! It is not you; it is my blind belief and trust in myself! I thought of myself to be above all weaknesses . . . This is a befitting punishment for my pride. But sometimes, it is too much to bear."

Cairo, December 16

Our conversation in the harbor brought me closer to Numan. I asked him how my nervous breakdown on that disastrous night affected Macide. Tearing up, he said: "Poor little woman! These kinds of things are so new to her that naturally, they turned her entire world upside down. The fact that she never suspected anything up until the last minute made the final blow even harder on her soul. But without a doubt she will overcome this."

"Do you think she will ever forgive me?"

"What have you done to be forgiven?"

"That's also true! But do you think I should write something to her?"

"That would be good."

Even though I want to question Numan about what happened with Seviyye that night, he is as hard as stone when it comes to talking about her. I begin to understand that he and my doctor have agreed to do everything possible to make me forget the cause of my illness. And they think this will happen by not talking about her? No, I will not forget her. Perhaps I'll learn to live with this pain but that is all!

The orderly streets and the festive life in Egypt felt a little strange to me. I see debauchery everywhere, a life without love and emotion! What is it about the treacherous bosom of the green Nile? What is in this ocean of golden sand burning under the sun? You, the woman with the mysterious smile, you the stone sculpture waiting in the middle of this golden, infinite desert for centuries, do you hold the key for heavenly pleasures in this land?

December 23

Today, after much deliberation, I finally wrote to Macide. For some time now, I have been testing my strength. I truly wish for every word in my letter to be an absolute pledge and to be ready to face death to keep it.

My precious friend Macide:

That day, next to my mother's deathbed, I had become yours forever. This bond was very sacred and dear to me. It still is. You have to believe that, come what may, I love you with all my heart, beyond any fleeting desire or tragedy. The recent events may be the best witness to my love because even when that unbearable nervous breakdown took away my health, I did not lose my affection for you. I have not violated your rights in any way.

I would like to stand in front of you like I would stand in front of God, with a naked soul. Listen: I loved Seviyye but not in the way that I love you; I loved her with a kind of passion that drowns one in darkness and shame, but I never told her anything, not even in moments when I thought I was about to go mad. I knew deep inside she was an honorable woman and that she would reproach me for declaring my love in that way. But I guess I would probably act the same way if it were any other kind of woman. In the end, my feelings were unrequited, but I had every opportunity. I am not saying this to defend myself. I owe this strength to my affection for you. Your pure and sacred heart lent me its helping hand. Your impeccable morals put me to shame.

I now see this second suffering, the kind that your innocent heart would not understand, as some kind of a tragedy and affliction. I will fight with all my heart to beat this sickness. In this, too, it is your little loving hands that help me. Be my lover, my dear friend, my nurturing nurse again! This is undoubtedly the only way to rip these wicked emotions from my heart.

After writing these words to you, I feel calmer and more at ease. I am not asking for your forgiveness because I remained loyal to you, as much as any human being can. And now I promise you this: When I return to Istanbul, I will never see Seviyye again. Even if there is an opportunity to see her, I will avoid it no matter what. I will not come back to Istanbul without being absolutely sure of myself. I guess you will not think it's possible that my heart can be torn in two like this, but time will prove it to you.

Won't you please send me a few words of affection? What a big comfort this would be for me.

Your Fahir

I kept thinking for a while after I finished the letter. I wondered if I would be able to keep my promise. No doubt every single word in the letter was true. No one else could ever give me the comfort, happiness, trust, and faith that I had found in little Macide's black eyes. She offered me a tranquil life, a peaceful soul, while the other, fire and poison. One was sensibility, the other, madness.

December 31

Curious and restless, I count the mail delivery days. I wonder if Macide will reply. At the same time, Numan and I lead a seemingly good life in Cairo. Theatre plays, balls, operas! Numan is taking advantage of it all, but there is such deep discontent in my soul for these things.

January 7

Today, I received a letter from Macide. It reads as follows:

Dear Fahir,

I wept for a long time when I received your letter. I have been wounded so deeply that nothing can bring me happiness in this world again, not even the love you offer to me as charity. You offer me, the woman who loves you with all her heart, only the love of a sibling, a friend.

I don't know what to say. But I know, after all this, I'll always feel like a widow. Fahir my friend, the Fahir I love so much may return one day, but Fahir my husband, the Fahir I imagined to be my lover, that Fahir will never come back!

Why am I telling you all these things like a fool? The truth is, I pray every night, lying in bed, looking at the empty space next to me, that you will come back to me, that things will be the way they were. Who knows, maybe my prayers will be heard, right? Try and get better soon because I cannot stand being alone for too long. Hikmet asks about you every day.

Fahir, are we in a dream? When will that woman stop casting her
shadow between us?

Macide

The woeful cry at the end of this child's letter has such dignified
solemnities . . . I almost feel a profound yearning to be with her. But,
no, I am not strong enough, not yet.

January 21

I received three more letters from Macide. These were filled with
little details about their lives, what she does and what she is reading.
I frequently think about the life in the little house in Çamlıca. Every
time I open a letter, I expect to see Seviyye's name. Even a complaint
about her would be welcome, but not a word.

I am getting weary of my meaningless life here. I am beginning to
understand that no distance will ever help me forget her. If only
there was a force to drag my mind and soul to the right path, then
I'd be able to forget.

January 23

I didn't leave the hotel today. I am afflicted with such suffocating
restlessness that I decided to return to Istanbul at once.

January 24

After a sleepless night, I pulled my chair to the window and watched the outside world. The Khedive Hotel itself overlooks a rather narrow street but at the end of that is the beginning of a major boulevard. I must have slept rather deeply after dawn because I didn't hear the breakfast bell. The door that opens to Numan's room is left ajar. I haven't yet seen him this morning.

I don't know whether or not I should ring the bell to ask for hot water.

My mind is obsessed with unknotting this grave emotional turmoil. This irresolvable weakness seems to follow me everywhere. It would be better, then, if I return home to my son instead of running away from life, being dragged into a life of decadence against my will, like a frightened child, right? Perhaps time, perhaps grey hair will one day make me forget all this madness. But how will I go on living until that moment? Perhaps the fact that Macide knows about my love for Seviyye and the promise I made to Macide will protect me from another madness.

While I was lost in these thoughts, Numan walked in quietly. He looked rather cheerful. He said he received a letter from Samime saying she was always by Macide's side. Eventually, he added with his usual indiscretion: "I have one last piece of good news for you."

"What's that?"

"Your aunt is very sick."

I immediately asked for the letter. He took out a letter without the envelope from his pocket.

"You go ahead and read the letter. I have to go downstairs. I had promised Miss Adeline a book."

"But, Numan, you are not behaving."

"Why, then we compete with each other in that."

"Have you seen me flirt with anyone since I got married?"

"O wish I had. You would not have been in this situation!"

Perhaps Numan was right. Perhaps the tragedies of the heart always find people like me who lead pure and chaste lives.

After Numan left, I started reading Samime's letter. It was written on a thick, cream-colored paper emanating an intimate, heavy violet scent. The stationary had little in common with Samime's taste. As soon as I read the opening line, "My Brother Numan!" I immediately realized that he gave me the wrong letter. First, I thought it must be from one of his siblings then I looked at the signature and there it was, "Seviyye."

With its entire white, splendid, magnificent magic, a part of her was finally in my hands. I was shivering, trying to stop myself from crying. For a few seconds, the letter rested on my knees. I was intoxicated with this beguiling piece of paper that her fingers had caressed and that her heart had touched, and eventually surrendered my body and soul to this prodigious feeling. And then suddenly, one of the sentences I had recently written to Macide in my letter stabbed my conscience! "After I return to Istanbul, I will never see Seviyye again. Even if there is an opportunity to see her, I will avoid it no matter what." How long had it been since I had written that sentence? I had promised in that letter that I would avoid Seviyye. Yes, but had I promised that I would run away from her letters? Besides, I had said "After I return to Istanbul" in my letter. So, I could actually be with her now, in spirit. All of a sudden, I heard my conscience cry out: "You hypocrite! How low can you get? You know very well that if you thought about the possibility of seeing Seviyye or her letters here, you would have promised that you would sincerely avoid them. You are trying to run away from moral responsibility like petty people do with their petty tricks. Don't you even have the courage to act indecent and call it that?"

At that moment, a shiver ran down my body. As I held this piece of paper in my hand, I felt utterly weak and miserable. If I could resist this very first temptation, this beguiling, gilded temptation that keeps pulling me back, perhaps I will be able to take the first step towards keeping my promise, otherwise this first step will only be to fall back.

I immediately locked up the letter in the drawer with shaky hands. If and how much I can resist the temptation to read this letter will be the true measure of whether my illness is improving or getting worse. I dressed up quickly and rushed out without telling Numan about it and jumped on the first tram to Giza. Awed by the golden infinity of the desert that strips humanity into nothingness, I sat under the stones that waited on the dead and I mused on. But they, too, kept their stubborn silence and did not reveal the secrets of life.

January 28

I never thought I'd have another woman's name on the pages of my diary. But now, I sense that this third woman will shape a part of my life as well. Why? Only because of her resemblance to the other!

Last night, Numan and I went out after dinner. Not knowing how we wanted to spend the night, we started promenading. Right then on the boulevard, I noticed a tall Brit exiting a brightly lit clothing store. I recognized him right away. He was Fred Leslie, our classmate at Oxford. When he saw us on the poorly lit street, he first hesitated then ran up to us enthusiastically: "Good evening old chap!" He said to Numan, "What are you doing in Egypt? I thought you were in Istanbul, busy looking for a wife among the newly uncaged Turkish women."

"That's right. But what's the point of being nailed to Istanbul after you find what you are looking for?," I replied.

"How about you, Fahir? You are a family man. Weren't you the only one in our class who was married with a child? What are you doing here? Or are you chasing an Egyptian woman?"

"My dear Fred. You treat us like we are world famous Casanovas. Have you seen us do anything in Oxford that makes you say these things?"

"I don't know about you but Numan went down to London quite frequently. You, old philosopher, I know how very earnest a man you are."

Numan was cracking up: "You are wrong, Fred. This time, we are traveling to the four corners of the world so that he can forget his lovesickness."

Once he catches a clue, Fred never lets the matter go until he finds out what's going on. Thankfully, with a quick sign, I was able to silence the blabbering Numan and change the subject. But Fred was staring at me reverently, as if I were some kind of a hero. As we were departing, he said: "If Fahir has trouble forgetting, the best way is to let him have some fun. What are your plans for tonight?"

"We don't have any plans. Tell us if you have any. But I am begging you, please, no women involved."

"Well, well, there is piousness, too, I see. To the contrary, I never have plans without women in them."

"Then I won't be joining you."

"Let me finish! This is the perfect program for a family man like yourself. We'll go to the opera."

"What is the program?"

"We are not going for the program. We are going so we can see the most beautiful primadonna of Britain."

He started humming right away: "Like a rose, white and exquisite . . ." I recalled this piece with all its poison and fire. With a desire to run away from the days of longing and endless pain, I said "Come on, then, let's go."

We were in the orchestra seats. Numan was as heedless and happy as a child. They were putting on *Faust*. More so than this beautiful opera which we had seen many times before, we were all waiting for the primadonna, described as the most beautiful in Britain. One person behind me was describing this new opera star as the "British Venus". No doubt opera is an imaginary, enchanting but—in the end—false representation of real life. These people who are suffering on stage under bright lights, covered with make-up, in their ornate costumes, singing and acting; how distant they are to the painful realities of our lives. Ah, how tonight's performance took me back to a moment in our childhood. How I wish I could just close my eyes and see little Seviyye sitting next to me, a boy in his school uniform, and on stage the old primadonna of Petit-Champs in her blue costume.

When Marguerite arrived on stage, there was a wave of silent excitement in the whole room. The pale Marguerite with her thick golden braids falling on her shoulders had suddenly slapped me in the face with her uncanny resemblance to Seviyye. Yes! If it weren't for the rosy, pinkish shadows on Marguerite's marvelous neck and naked shoulders, how I would have taken them to be the pale, marble-like shoulders of Seviyye. If we don't count her round face with its pinkish hue and perfect features, she had the same mysterious gaze hiding behind lily-like eye lids closing under a narrow forehead and brown eyebrows. How I adored those eyelids that opened and closed like a delicate lily. How they would mesmerize me, pull me to their mysterious depths with delightful shivers. Now, in this new country, this mystical atmosphere, in front of this beautiful woman who is graced with the shadow of the other, my open wounds bleed again, painfully, and I feel the black hands of a nervous breakdown creep into my soul after a month of healing.

Fred watched the primadonna with youthful love and longing. Numan whispered to me anxiously: "You look like you need some fresh air. Let's go."

"No. I would like to see her eyes."

Yes, finally, the eyelids I longed to see, even for a minute, the eyelids I would give up everything for were lifted, but alas, underneath were another pair of eyes: A pair of sweet, bright, happy, and seductive blue eyes! Where are those soft and dark chestnut eyes hiding such intense tragedies, such profound longing in their sweet hues?

January 29

Last night, I came back to the hotel in turmoil. That cruel master whom I wanted to destroy forever had knocked me on my feet with its old, insolent grandeur. I stood by the drawer for a few seconds before I changed my clothes, and in the end, I decided to read the letter. But right then Numan walked in.

"I was really worried. If she hadn't lifted her eyelids, this resemblance would have destroyed you. But tell me, those seductive, twinkling blue eyes immediately chased away Seviyye from your thoughts, right? You still look very pale Fahir. Are you ill?"

"I feel rather weak, my brother."

It was true. When I saw Numan, I had broken down like a child who gets saved from grave danger at the last minute. He turned the switch on, opened the door to his room, and started chatting as he changed his clothes.

"Undress and get in bed, Fahir. I'll be there shortly to read to you."

I obeyed him like a little child. All the fever and outbursts I anticipated
had melted away with this sickly and infernal despair for now.

January 30

Numan's voice woke me up from a long, feverish, and uneasy dream.

"You lucky dog! Look who sent you an invitation."

He held a thick envelope to my sleepy eyes. This was Fred's
handwriting. He then took out a letter from the already opened
envelope and read it in a teasing but cheerful tone:

> *Old friends,*
>
> *Yesterday, I received a letter from Evelyn Marshall, the primadonna.*
> *I know her from England. She is a wonderful girl. She is under Lord*
> *Stanley's (one of my friends) wings. There are even rumors about a*
> *marriage, but Evelyn loves her freedom and is in no rush. Apparently,*
> *the other night, she was intrigued by the dark-haired young Turk*
> *next to me, whom she thought looked like Pietro Mascagni. She is*
> *talking about Fahir, of course. Now, she is inviting both of you here*
> *for tea. I am sending the invitation. It is beyond me how she'd prefer*
> *to add a gloomy man like Fahir to her exquisite British collection.*
> *What can I say, women!*
>
> *In envy of Fahir,*
> *Fred*

"How now? You are not saying anything, Fahir. Does that mean you are not accepting the invitation?"

"I don't know."

"If you ask me, don't miss out on this opportunity. If you continue to be a gloomy owl crying for the past, you'll never heal."

"What would you have me do?"

"Live a little, use your ability to love to get rid of the poison in your heart."

"Oh, I see. You are advising treachery."

"How is it treachery? If it can take you back to Macide in one piece it would not really be treacherous."

"Why not? Being supremely in love with Seviyye would be treachery, but being a love toy in Evelyn Marshall's hands wouldn't be shameful, right?"

"Come on, now. You don't think a woman who invites you to tea will just throw herself at you, do you? But then what if she were to!"

"Then let's just go back to Istanbul and I shall declare my love to Seviyye!"

"But you are forgetting that she is an honorable woman."

"Are you sure?"

"If I didn't love you as a brother, I would put a bullet in your head right now."

"You would have destroyed a head much deserving of that."

Regretful and caring, Numan held my hands tightly and didn't mention Evelyn Marshall's name again until dinner.

But at four thirty we were both dressed up handsomely, walking in the direction of Shepheard Hotel.

At the hotel, we were taken into a luxurious room. Lord Stanley, Fred, two Brits, and a young Egyptian gentleman named Aziz Bey were in the room. Miss Evelyn greeted us in a plain but tastefully embroidered blue dress. She was a tall, beautiful, a very beautiful woman. Her ever bright, smiling blue eyes, her elegant laughter on the curve of her red lips enslaved and mesmerized all men in the room. They were all in her orbit. The only man who was cold and uninterested in the room was me. The primadonna on stage with her blonde braids and downcast eyes was gone, there was nothing here to remind me of Seviyye. I got up to leave before everyone else. "Have you seen the pyramids?" she asked impatiently as I was getting ready to leave.

"Yes, Miss."

"I haven't. I would have loved to visit them with someone who knows their history. Fred told me that you know ancient Egyptian history quite well."

"I am at your service, Miss Marshall."

"Stanley, send your car in at half past three tomorrow."

Lord Stanley frowned but was quickly disarmed by the joyful, blue might exuding from Miss Marshall's eyes; "All right, Evelyn" he said, defeated.

February 1

Fred left the hotel with us. "If only you knew how much you have impressed Evelyn, Fahir!"

"Fred, my friend, the man who turns a cold shoulder to a woman, who looks down upon everyone is naturally treated as an eccentric animal."

"Is this the new politics of the new Turkey?"

"No, but it is the politics of the new Turks!"

"I am guessing that you fell in love with a magnificent Turkish queen, and you don't have eyes for anyone else but her!"

"Never mind Fahir's stale past now and tell us what Miss Evelyn said about Fahir."

"Well, I don't know. She compares Fahir to all the classical Italians there are out there. Before you arrived, all she could talk about was his hair and his eyes."

"Well, Fred, you are giving me a reason to look in the mirror."

Indeed, when I went back to my room, I looked in the mirror. If I had the looks to attract women, could it be that I occupied Seviyye's dreams, even a little? But the imploring black eyes that I saw in the mirror looked so sick and weary.

The following day, I got ready and arrived at the Shepheard Hotel at three thirty to take Evelyn to the pyramids with a strange torment and curiosity in my soul. There was Miss Evelyn, in a tight and beige-colored dress, wearing a large, strange-looking hat and a long and soft tulle shawl for the ride. With her tight street costume, and the yellow shadows of the hat that framed her elegant face, she was no doubt the most beautiful British woman I had ever seen. In my soul, however, was nothing but indifference towards her joyful blue eyes.

Shepheard's Hotel, Cairo, Courtesy of the Rare Books and Special Collections Library, The American University in Cairo.

We were driving through roads lined with trees on both sides, over bridges on the bluish green of the Nile. I felt ready for a new and peaceful feeling to rise within me. In the meantime, my companion was observing me like a cunning commander, busy with the conquest of a castle. Coquettish and seductive one minute, and indifferent the next, she was trying to enchant me with her ever-changing moods. Women of the theatre can create such varied illusions for the men they desire; they can put on such different and pleasant masks that sooner or later you fall for one of them, but I could see through these games with all their subtleties and artificialities. As we got closer to the pyramids, I finally rebelled against how this new barbarian machine we were riding cut through the glorious slumber of the desert, awakening the centuries, "Evelyn, let's leave this crazy new machine here and go to the desert on foot, shall we?" I said.

"All right. I wish we had dressed up in traditional Arab clothes. Shall we ride the camel?"

"I always find it quite ridiculous to ride a camel with a hat or even a fez! No doubt that the children of the desert who protect their old traditions under their loose garments laugh at us bitterly every time."

"Right."

We walked in the desert, arm in arm: a woman ready to betray and a reluctant man. The first act of this love affair must have picked the silent vastness of the immortal desert as its stage. Who knows how many tragedies or comedies Cleopatra's mysterious sand dunes must have witnessed!

The setting sun had covered the yellow sand, the distant villages, and even the air with a light rosy color. Evelyn's feint flirtations were silenced in the presence of this sublime mystery. The artist in her was consumed and humbled by the sublime silence of this infinite desert, a subtle reminder of the dawn of time. Then gently she started singing in a reverie, hesitant to disturb the eternity around her. Her high soprano tones lacked the sincerity and tragedy that would shake me to my core and bring me close to death, like that voice I left behind, on the other side of the sea. And yet it revealed such a masterful range, taking on such different colors and shapes. Forlorn, composed, mysterious, it was as if she whispered her words, "A jug of wine, a loaf of bread, and thou/ Beside me singing in the Wilderness/ O, Wilderness were Paradise now!"

People change, places and frames change but, suffering, heartache and poets remain forever unchanged.

I bent over and lifted the thin tulle covering her face. She looked pale under the yellow-pink desert colors. The seductive gaze was gone, her brown brows looked a little furrowed, her lips tight, and I could see Seviyye's lily eyelids on that beautiful face, subdued by the dawning melancholy and sheathing nothingness of the desert, imbued with her mysteries.

Unable to control the madness in my voice, I said to her: "Evelyn, always keep your gaze down, won't you?"

On the way back, her rosy complexion was ablaze with victorious flames; her youthful eyes were smiling as always, but this time content with a new feeling. I believe this woman assumes I love her but that I am somehow inhibited by my oriental shyness. That means, by remaining silent, I was deceitful. Of course, I had to act in an extremely distant manner the following day to erase that impression.

February 18

I have spent the last fifteen days between the Cairo Opera House and
the Shepheard Hotel. I admit I have a rather trivial connection to this
new woman who occupies my every minute and never leaves me
alone. There is more like a battle between us: not yet having added
me to her army of slaves, she chases me with her chain in hand and
I upset her with long, distant silences that follow brief moments of
weakness I show whenever she reminds me of Seviyye. She gets quite
irritated with my resistance and to hide her anger, she bestows even
more attention on me. I don't know how this battle will end. Feasts,
banquets, theatre plays take up all my time. After midnight, when
we return to the hotel room, I rest my head on the cold window
glass for a few minutes and weary of this new life, I wish to end it
all. But in the morning, when I wake up, the promise of a new lunch
date or a promenade makes me forget everything. Numan is rather
content with this situation. He must have written to Macide about
me because I received a bittersweet letter from her. She says she is
delighted that I am enjoying life and trying my best to forget about
everything, but in her poor, young, loving, faithful heart, there is
doubt and suspicion . . .

I am holding her letter in my hand. Tonight, my mind is on Macide.
How much longer am I to torment this child who is wasting the best
years of her youth alone, missing someone. The best thing to do is no
doubt to put an end to this comedy and return back home. Seviyye's
memories could not be more cruel in Istanbul than they already
are here. Besides, I am a man with a life sentence and this pain that

burns my very being ever so fiercely, ever so infinitely will even follow me to the afterlife. I no longer desire this empty, spurious life that I have been living only to put out the flames in my soul. So, I wrote to Evelyn and told her that I wasn't coming. After all, wasn't it Seviyye's shadow on her that I was chasing?

Numan, ignorant of the reasons behind my relapse into melancholy looked baffled. He came to my room after dinner.

"I don't understand you at all, Fahir. The most beautiful woman in the world is courting you, and you are still thinking about that woman who is nothing but a dream."

"I am not thinking about her."

"Who are you thinking about then?"

"Macide."

"Is that so!"

"Yes, I know that I am treating both Evelyn Marshall and Macide terribly. Evelyn thinks that she will always be victorious in her game. But the truth is far from that. I am around her only to see the shadows of a woman that I vowed to forget forever. Loving Seviyye meant betraying Macide, but that was still something human, something uncontrollable. I was at least true to myself. But what about this one? In this, I am betraying myself, Macide, and no matter how treacherous it may be, I am also betraying the love who taught me about betrayal. The right thing to do is to pack and go to Macide. It is not like I'd be more miserable than I am here!"

"You are insane, Fahir. I seriously don't get why you are acting so cold towards Evelyn. No doubt that you will be rejecting the world's most beautiful woman now."

"Don't rush to conclusions. Perhaps we believe in vain that this woman has fallen for me. It is just a flirtation. There is nothing between us yet!"

"I believe Evelyn loves you. I noticed recently that she has dark circles under her eyes, and how sad and irritable she looks. This is all because of your indifference to her."

"That's an unfortunate remark, Numan. Your imagination seems to be overworking tonight. I am happy to leave my place to you if you'd like."

Numan slammed the door in my face and left.

February 21

I haven't been to Evelyn's in three days. I am determined to have some certainty in my life, and I feel stronger than ever before, all thanks to Numan. Until now, I was the sick child and those around me were my caretakers. Now, it is my turn. I feel responsible for Numan. I notice that he is stirred with new feelings for Evelyn. That womanizer, talkative man all of a sudden became quiet and irritable. Most of the time, he is watching me with choleric eyes. If I don't get away from this sultry land of passion and danger, I will not only lose my willpower but also cause my friend's downfall. Sometimes, I can feel his envious gaze on me; it's devouring his soul. To see a woman's shadow cast on our life-long friendship, our brotherhood. Now, I cannot bear that pain . . .

Today, I went to the Cook Travel Agency and planned our travel. We will go back to Istanbul with the Romania Ferry that will leave Alexandria on February 28.

This time, I have to take the reins and drag Numan out of this.

February 22
I received a protesting letter from Evelyn last night saying how she doesn't understand my silence and how upset she is. She invites me to the opera and then to the Shepheard Hotel for a banquet. She says only then I'll be pardoned for neglecting her. I gave my invitation to Numan.

"Why don't you go? I feel a little unwell. Go in my place."

Numan's eyes shined for a moment but right away his face fell, "Who knows what these women are dragging us into," he said.

Numan came back late that night. He walked into my room quietly, but I pretended to be asleep.

February 23

This morning, Numan told me that Evelyn received him rather badly last night. He looked sad and surly.

"Let's return to our country, shall we?" I asked Numan.

Numan grabbed my hands fiercely and squeezed them.

"That's exactly what I wanted to tell you, but I didn't have the courage to do it. I also want to ask you something, but you'll be honest with me, right?"

"Do you ever doubt that?"

He leaned over to my ear and asked what I had expected to hear: "Never, my dear Numan. I swear. It was never more than a benign flirtation. Rest assured."

"Ah, women! They die not for those who love them but for their oppressors."

Numan and I had a long conversation that morning about our return and our future. The harmony and camaraderie had fully been restored to our friendship. That afternoon, we went for a walk together. When we got back, the custodian approached me and said that a British woman was looking for me. All of a sudden, Numan grew pale. I grabbed his arm and took him upstairs.

"Let's be strong. We will leave very soon," I said.

After dinner, we sat on the large seats in the public lounge and savored our cigarettes. I was lost in thoughts of our return in this smoke-filled room. I don't know why but I kept thinking about a young and beautiful woman, attending the sick bed of an ill-humored mother, tending to the child of a man who doesn't know how to be a dutiful father; of the worry in her loyal heart. No doubt, Macide must have put on one of those simple dresses that she used to wear as a young girl, sitting on the woven mat, listening to my aunt's harsh words. Who knows how this old woman must be poisoning her faith and affection, drop by drop.

As my mind was busy with these thoughts, the waiter approached me and said I had a phone call. I immediately sensed who it was. Taking advantage of Numan and Miss Adeline's heated conversation, I went to receive the call. I guess I didn't want to get Numan excited.

A shaky and passionate voice on the other side of the line started: "Fahir, listen to me and promise me that you'll do whatever I say, otherwise know that I'll come to your hotel."

I didn't know how to respond to this woman's offhand style. We weren't even that close. She continued: "They said you were leaving in two days. Are you running away from me?"

"No, Miss Evelyn. I am going back to my family," I said.

"Don't philosophize. I have a headache. You must come at once to end this war between us."

"To where?"

"Shepheard Hotel. I will be by myself after the play. Stanley is in Alexandria. Don't you dare bring your chaperon Numan with you."

"All right, Miss. Evelyn."

What else could I do but accept this invitation. Besides, I was already disarmed by this beautiful woman's courage, which had put us in such an arcane and absolute situation. I could sense that I was about to resolve things that were yet unbeknownst to me about life, about existence. I grabbed my coat and fez, and without saying a word to anyone, I left.

March 2

I am completing my memoir in the dining hall of the boat. As soon as I return to Istanbul, I will have these sealed and hand them to a bank safe box, only to be opened by my son Hikmet when he turns twenty-two years old.

So much has transpired over the last couple of days that I feel as if my soul is drowning in a sea of pain and sorrow. I am drifting away from everyone. Death is slowly creeping into every part of my existence. This demise is not only spiritual but material. I feel that my brain, the source of all my thoughts and emotions, is rotting and that I am willingly and idly losing my youth in a downfall. In the last few days, strange colors and dark shadows float in front of my eyes.

I would have wanted to preserve this big love affair as a big love affair and also stay true to the people around me. But I understand now that not even a thousand souls can stand the flames of such a fire. Perhaps the best thing was never to fight against the forces of nature. I used up my last bit of strength at the Shepheard Hotel. I left Egypt as I entered it, that is, with untouched loyalty to Macide. But I have fallen ill.

I remember that very last night with all its details. When I arrived at the Shepheard Hotel, Evelyn's femme de chambre greeted me. She walked with me across the hall and escorted me to Evelyn's bedroom, as if I was the secret owner of that apartment.

"Madame asked that you wait for her here. If you need anything, please call me," she said and left the room.

Even though I wanted to tell her that I'd rather wait in the hall, I didn't want to look unversed and ludicrous in front of Evelyn's femme de chambre. So, I walked into the room with a feigned ease.

This room was turned into a warm and soft nest of pleasure quite intentionally, or maybe it was my inexperience that easily made me intoxicated by the scent of romance in this soft corner. Across from a white bed sitting under a canopy of white tulles was a big, soft divan. The rather inviting bed was covered with many soft and colorful pillows. Next to it was a huge, deep armchair with a big rose-colored silk throw on it and cushions in the same color, and a precious leather rug in front of the armchair. This place said Evelyn in every way. But there was more, a faint scent in her armchair, the gloves left on her vanity desk, the tiny white slippers under her bed, the lace and muslin nightgown on the chair that took on the contours of her body . . . All these objects brought fragrant, beautiful, and irresistible waves from her to me.

The only lamps that spread a pinkish hue in the air were the rose-petal colored night lamps. The main lights were not switched on. It was as if a faded pink light cast its shadow on the secrets of the heart in this corner. I sat there and contemplated until Evelyn arrived. I was mostly analyzing myself. Since I walked into this room, I felt like a different Fahir. I realize that there can be relationships that have nothing to do with the heart and thoughts governed only by animal instinct. In fact, a person's body can be governed by reason, he can be enslaved by the love of another's face, and still lose himself under these influences. But already my nerves were tightening, my will power was arming up, and getting ready to shield itself. On the other hand, I was thinking how sweet it would be to lie down in that soft and warm corner and bury all my pain and madness . . .

The life I lived with the prudence of a virgin girl and my virtuous life until now flashed before my eyes. What a dignified, innocent, virtuous life it was. But that wasn't enough to tie my heart and my conscience to where it belonged, my wife. In the first fire I faced, I lost my very self. My God, what have I done, what is it that I did that makes me feel so sick at heart and mind, and live in perpetual torment just so that I stay loyal to the purity of my past. I believe my only mistake was to think that I was above anyone else, more virtuous than anyone. Such selfish arrogance. I feel such tremendous hatred towards the old, proud Fahir in me now. After these long nights, unending sorrows, and calamities, I feel such pity in my heart for humanity's damnable weaknesses, its most terrible flaws.

I heard a soft and loving voice whisper, "Tonight, I am Marguerite again." I must have been so lost in my own thoughts as I hadn't even heard the changing room door open. I turned my head. The silhouette at the door was quite charming. Evelyn was wearing a peignoir as delicate as a rose petal, over her loose shirt. The lace and muslin peignoir barely covered her legs. I could see her knees and elegant feet. Her beautiful shoulders and neck were completely naked and the two blonde braids she had for the show were falling down on her shoulders. Her face looked a little tired but more meaningful than

ever before. If the queen of love in this mysterious land had arisen
from the dead and was resurrected amidst these mysterious, pinkish
shadows, she could not have been more attractive than Evelyn.

How far removed she was from coquetry and dominance. She
reached for her slippers from under her bed and reclined on the
divan. Then rather casually, she started to talk and put on her slippers
at the same time. Her feet reminded me of the water lilies of the Nile.
Her eyelids looked so heavy, her voice was so low that I thought this
solemn, cold body was actually hiding another woman, the one who
was pulling the strings of my heart from the other side of the sea. My
temples were about to explode, as if to tell me that despite my past
victory, my illness was invading me with a vengeance. Evelyn was
always talking. She looked so weary of everything that I assume she
doesn't have a personal plan for me tonight!

"If only you knew how tired I feel, Fahir. You may think I invited you to
my bedroom for personal reasons. No, a thousand times no! To be
loved, to be wealthy, to have the world under my feet, even to become
a great Lady . . . these are things I can easily get. Even putting my
heart and soul out in the open every night to an army of strangers,
seeing thousands of people worshipping me, is insignificant. All I
really want is to be understood, only to be understood and to have
a relationship that's selfless, reciprocal, and affectionate. Do you
understand me?"

She lifted up her blue eyes. There was something extraordinary in these blue lights that delved deep into the pink void. I shivered. I thought for a moment that the colors, light, scents, an invisible net in this beautiful woman's beautiful body was about to trap my willpower. When she noticed my silence, she put her head on the pillows and closed her eyes. Her lips repeated the same cries and moans about love and tragedy. All of a sudden, those lily eyelids took me back to the nest behind the green leaves in Çamlıca. Seviyye was there in front of me, like a marble statue with a golden, soft contour, like the last time I saw her. I could see her wide shoulders narrowing down, making a curve, her white, pale complexion, and pale hair. She was asleep. Her eyes closed, resting under her peaceful brown eyelashes and her eyebrows. But as soon as these deadly white lilies were lifted, the eyes that captured my soul, the pleasures of love that I had buried deep inside me erupted, set my soul aflame. I slowly crawled to Evelyn's knees, looked into those eyes which breathed life into my beloved across the sea, and worshipped them with all my heart and soul . . . then something deep inside me moved my lips to her eyelids, to reunite with her. Another minute and our souls would embrace in eternal ecstasy. At that moment, with the mightiness and grandeur of my bliss, I would join the world of the gods and disappear. The next thing I recall is that I was pushing away this woman, who gave wings to my dreams with her blue eyes, violently by her shoulders. She fell on the armchair. I was crying, screaming, laughing hysterically, going mad. I was calling out my fleeting beloved, begging her: "Seviyye, Seviyye, Seviyye!"

How the pain in my voice echoed with golden waves in this pink chamber of pleasures. I was on Evelyn's divan. I felt a woman rubbing my stiff arms and dabbing eau de cologne on my temples. It was almost dawn. There was affection in Evelyn's teary blue eyes.

"So, there was another woman? Poor, poor, Fahir!" she said gently.

I returned from that room ill and broken. Numan had been waiting for me in my room all night long, wondering where I was, walking the streets to find me. I told him everything. I was now at the end of my strength and patience. After all the fights I had put up, all the wars I had waged on my soul, nothing had worked. All my fights were in vain. I was going to go back to Istanbul and beg for Seviyye's love like a wretched man.

With a sad and downcast expression, Numan told me that nothing could ever happen between Seviyye and me.

"I had received a letter from Seviyye. I hadn't told you about it. Wait, I'll bring it . . ."

"Don't go. I have that letter."

"How? Did you steal the letter from me, Fahir?"

"No. You had given it to me saying that it was from Samime. But, I haven't read it yet."

I pointed at the drawer. He opened it, took out Seviyye's letter, and started reading it:

My brother Numan,

I have good news for you, but considering the circumstances under which you have left and knowing how terrible a time you must be going through I cannot bring myself to say it. After you left, our case with Talip Bey was resolved. I am free and can do as I please now. Think about it, Numan. Now I can go out in the world without that seal of shame on my forehead. I am now in my father's house. In fifteen days, Cemal and I will get married. This is such great happiness that only you, who have stood by me throughout the calamities of my life, would understand.

Macide Hanım abandoned the piano classes right after you left. She doesn't even greet me on the street now. But so what? When you think of my new happiness, this is nothing, right? I am writing to cheer you up. I am also quite upset that you will not be at my wedding.

How is the patient? I hope that when he returns, he will be well enough to be happy for me. Send me news from Egypt.

Your sister,
Seviyye

Seviyye was now another man's wife, the man she loved! First, I
regretted terribly that I didn't read the letter as soon as I found it.
Seviyye, a divorcee and on her own! Who knows, perhaps, perhaps,
it could have been me, I thought to myself; such a dizzying thought!
Then she wished me to be well enough to feel happy for her. This
stabbed me in the heart. What did it mean anyway? I guess she wants
me to be indifferent to her. I guess I am nothing compared to him; I
am simply worthless, right? "That's enough" I said to Numan "Let's
not talk about this woman anymore. Tomorrow, we are heading to
Alexandria."

March 5

We arrived in Istanbul today. This is the second time in the last year
that I arrive in my country.

The first one was after July, in the first months of liberation. At that
time, this country was flapping its wings with such high aspirations
and ideals. Everyone was busy sowing the seeds of the new Turkey
that was reorganizing itself. Today, I see a spiritual connection
between the state of my country and myself. Back then, I, too, had
started life with a clear plan in mind. Now, the political party debates,
the spreading seditions of the infectious and impossible-to-eradicate
groups, the erosion of morality have all turned the country into a
war zone. A threatening growl hovers in the air, people are mutinous,
willing to do something extreme.

My eyes searched for a charshaf and a little boy on the pier but there was nobody. For a second time Macide hadn't come to meet me. I recalled my thoughts at the *Sirkeci Station* that day, on my first return to Istanbul. How childish they were. How far removed was I now from that hopeful and ambitious young Fahir from eight months ago. Numan and I quietly walked up to *Üsküdar. Çamlıca* streets looked a bit dustier, the sidewalks looked a bit more rickety. When the carriage stopped in front of the house, a little blond child ran inside calling, "Mother." Two minutes later, Macide appeared at the kitchen door. Compared to eight months ago, she, too, was a picture of sorrow. I had made this woman's soul age in a matter of months; my heart hurt from shame and regret. This time, we didn't throw ourselves into each other's arms; neither of us showed any excitement. Macide's eyes looked reddish and her young cheeks pale but there were no tears in her eyes now.

In an awkward joy amidst this grim silence, Numan said: "Here, Macide Hanım. I am returning him to you. The only thing for me to do now is to run to Samime and turn myself in to her."

After a quick goodbye, he jumped back on the carriage that drove us home and left.

March 8

The news of the assassination of the editor-in-chief of *Serbesti Newspaper* rattled the entire city. I, on the other hand, am strangely uninterested in politics now. I am thinking that those of us who were supposed to heal the country's sickness, its spirit, have failed bitterly and terribly. I am probably just one small example, a measure of this. I had returned from Europe to spread reform and happiness around me. I was going to change Macide's life, elevate her culturally. Alas! I changed her life but not by giving her a new source of happiness. Not only did I take away her existing peace and old beliefs, but I added nothing new to her life, thus leaving her with an affliction that made her restless, unsatisfied, empty-handed, abandoned, and confused. How could she ever trust me again, a man who is supposed to be a representative of a reformed new life? I now looked at the entire country as a bigger reflection of our own life. But the blame is neither on me nor on the reformists in the country. Our goodwill, efforts, and sacrifices were shattered before human weaknesses and the incurable flaws of humanity.

Since the day I came back, I've felt something between Macide and me breaking down irreparably. I feel the coldness of death spreading to all the places where we spend time, including our bedroom. The night I came back, the marriage bed, a symbol of our warm, sincere married life, felt like a coffin to me.

Hikmet's crib was now enjoined by a little bed in the room. At bedtime, Macide said in a shaky voice, as she climbed up that bed: "Since you are tired, I asked they put another bed here, so we don't disturb you."

For a moment, she expected a revolt or imploration, but this time, I lacked the courage to be hypocritical towards this poor woman. I felt a deep gratitude towards her, but there was nothing other than regret and pity for her in my young, miserable, restless heart.

March 10

There is Spring in the air, it's spread to the mountains. Such beautiful, fresh, sunny days!

I find myself waiting for something that is not coming back. Most days, I am busy watching over Hikmet, who plays by himself on the street. Sometimes he looks at me with his big eyes as if to say how quiet the days are after the much-anticipated father arrived home, but then he goes back to play with his clay-dough house again.

For a few mornings, I found Macide busy, helping Hikmet with his homework. After she teaches him the letters of the alphabet for hours, she lectures him on other subjects. Her study desk is covered with English books on the education of children. She fills the void of her empty heart with the love of learning now and spends her days always with her reading and writing. When I look at her ever-thinning face, the sublime modesty I see keeps me from feeling sorry for her. In this calm and virtuous Macide, I now sense a great personality that I hadn't seen before. Yesterday morning, I eavesdropped on Hikmet's lesson. Macide was trying to ingrain in the child a story she called "the purpose of life." She said that the purpose of life was to be brave, faithful, true to yourself, honorable, and courageous. "But not just with guns and cannons, you will also learn to be brave with your will: You will be brave enough to not commit bad acts, brave enough to do what you believe is right, even if they threaten to kill you, my son. Always, always be true to yourself, do you understand Hikmet? Even if this kills others and cuts open and crushes their hearts, even if it tortures the person you love, you'll stay true to yourself! Do you understand Hikmet?"

Then, with a sob-like whisper, she added: "Just, just like your father!"

I left the house before tears started streaming down my face and ran up to the mountains.

March 11
Last night, I dreamt about Seviyye! It felt so very real. She came near my bed in a white nightgown. With her piercing eyes, she looked right into my eyes, my soul, my wounds . . . These healing eyes unlocked the cruel knots of my life. My soul ascended to the heavens through a glaring light.

March 12
All day, I shivered. Macide told me that I looked pale and that my hands felt warm. She said I needed bed rest. But I still wandered into the hills.

March 15

Today, Numan and Samime visited us. Even they were unusually quiet. Numan wasn't as chatty as he usually is. Samime looked sad. I see that poor Numan was also saved from a precipitous fall in the last moment. It is as if he had brushed danger and passed through it. I congratulated myself for leaving Egypt right on time. I would have never forgiven myself if Numan, too, suffered from what has turned my youth and my character into ashes. But a voice in my head kept saying "How dare you pull away the one thing everyone deserves to feel at least once in their lifetime?" Would it have been better to leave him there as a slave to Evelyn Marshall's blue eyes?

April 2

It was such a beautiful day that I wanted to spend the whole day on the thyme-covered hills. With Spring, there emerged in me hope, a fresh excitement that wants to resurface; a desire to reunite my life with Macide again! But I don't have the courage to say to that dignified, modest woman, "Let's belong to each other like we did in the past." I know how this will give her youth and happiness back. Sometimes, I see such sorrow and longing in her black eyes that my heart aches with bitter regret.

Yesterday, I inquired about my aunt—something I had neglected to do since I returned. Tears appeared in Macide's eyes. I understood. I felt ashamed of how self-absorbed I was with my own suffering and my inadvertent heedlessness and forgetfulness. So now this poor young woman had no one other than me in life. I made a gesture to pull her withering head to my chest, but she said in a wounded manner: "No! I don't want your pity. I can tolerate everything but not that, Fahir, do you understand me! This would be your biggest and final insult to me."

Then, with a smile on her face, as if nothing happened, she said calmly: "The weather is beautiful. Wouldn't you like to go out and walk a little bit?"

Neither of us slept last night. I know that I need to rip this desire from my heart if I ever want to go back to Macide. Offering her a broken, partial affection would mean offering her less than her worth. I lay in bed without saying a single word to her. A little before dawn, I heard what sounded like sobs coming from her bed, but, alas, I knew there was nothing to be done.

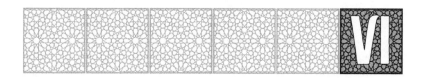

The Abyss

April 3

I was walking on the road when I saw Seviyye and Cemal head towards the green bushes that I always avoided. I felt a sharp pain stir up my heart. I tried to flee right away but there wasn't enough time. Seviyye turned to Cemal and whispered something in his ear, then they both turned and greeted me. I couldn't see Seviyye's eyes but she blushed. I, too, greeted them courteously, then left.

April 10

My old melancholic days are now coming to an end. Like a mad person, I keep spying on that house behind the green bushes. Who knows how much lower I will go. As they walk by me with the affection and love of new couples, I sacrifice everything for her eyes.

April 12

It was such a stifling and heavy night that we all woke up feeling tired and uneasy. Dazed, as if I woke up from a nightmare, I left the bed quite late.

Macide was feeling a little unwell. I could hear her call after Hikmet with a weary voice all day. I have no idea how time passed and the evening arrived. After dinner, I went up to the hills again to get some fresh air. My nerves are suffocated under a dense, stagnant oppression, the kind that brings wild storms.

At night, I wander idly as if I am in a dream. After walking around for half an hour, something outside of my control took me to the house behind the green bushes. I went there and opened the garden gate quietly, and entered, not knowing why I went there in the first place. I told myself, "This is just a visit. Besides, I would like to show Seviyye that I am not weak." But my soul, crying helplessly with contempt and defeat, knew it was being dragged into the abyss. And this is what I wanted. I wanted to fall into the abyss and disappear; that was my heart's sweet desire.

I knocked gently. The old maid came to the door with the lamp in her hand. She looked surprised to see me: "The Bey is at the neighbor's house. He will come back late. Hanım went to bed."

"Accept me into the living room. I must see the Bey. I will wait until he returns."

"Unfortunately, there is no fire in the living room."

"Not a problem. It is warm tonight."

"All right then, come in. Shall I let the Hanım know?"

First, I was going to say, yes, let her know. Then, thinking that she might decline to see me, I said: "No, don't bother her."

I shivered with maddening memories as I watched the objects around me. Why was I here? It wasn't to see Cemal, that was certain. I guess I was here to witness my own downfall, my own tragedy. I was here to see the objects she lived with, touch them with my hands. This was worth dying for!

I went up to the piano and rested my head on the edge where Seviyye rests her arm when she sings, and I waited. This piece of wood brought me back her sweet-smelling essence and penetrated right into my soul.

"Eleni, who is downstairs? I heard voices."

"Nothing. There is a guest here to see the Bey."

"I don't know when the Bey will come home tonight. Please don't make the guest wait."

"It is no stranger. It is Fahir Bey."

Footsteps were getting closer to the door. With every step, she was crushing my heart. Now, another minute and I would be right in front of her, all alone in the same house . . . My God!

The footsteps stopped. The hand on the door handle paused for a moment, a moment that felt like eternity. Finally, she walked in. I lifted my eyes to see in her my destiny. She was wrapped in a plain, blue cotton robe de chambre. She was covering her neckline with one hand and holding the candleholder with the other. Her eyes were downcast as usual, but she was frowning, with red angry spots appearing on her face. She had the rightful revolt of an honorable, married woman.

"Cemal will not come home tonight!"

"The maid said he was at the neighbor's house."

"Did you come here for Cemal?"

My whole existence was shaken by the possible meanings behind this question. In a helpless and weak voice, I said: "No."

She paused for a few seconds and in a low voice, she said: "Then please leave."

This humiliation struck such a big blow to the deepest and most secret corners of my existence that I suddenly lost my mind. I walked towards the door, burning with enough rage and pain to tear this woman who had turned my life upside down, into pieces. I was dying to see that pale, short, blue-eyed teacher with a vile envy and wrath. I was going mad, quaking with the desire to see him, so much so that I was scared of the things I could do to him if he were in front of me. There was only one thing in front of my eyes, a bloody spot; it was Cemal's severed head in the house, covered in blood. This is such a vision that it crushed my love under foot.

Seviyye asked with a fearful voice: "Where are you going? Are you going to do something bad to Cemal?"

I had no more patience left in me. I grabbed the wrists of this woman who had made me live centuries worth of madness in a few months and said, with the enmity of a mad person: "Yes. You'll see it when I throw Cemal's crushed brain at your feet."

Without pulling her hands away, she lifted her eyes up. Like the forever thirsty desert sand, I felt life gushing into my burning soul. I felt a wild fear that I hadn't felt in even my most feverish, dark days. I saw the absolute submission in the fiery depths of Seviyye's eyes. Right at that moment, everything that could have saved me from the abyss had retreated. There was nothing left in the entire universe other than fire and light, and Seviyye.

April 16

The entire country is in turmoil with bloody uprisings and rabid attacks. The city has witnessed atrocities; people jumping at each other's throats, turning into beasts. Cannon balls, rifles, fire, and blood everywhere. I feel like I, too, will forever fall into the depths of the dark, like this fallen nation. How sinful, filthy, and wild a beast I am! While the entire country is losing blood, flames erupting in its heart, I, too, am burning in flames, fever, and pain. I walked myself into that dark abyss of a crime that I struggled so hard to avoid, tried so much to run away from, and I fell right into it.

Everywhere I look, I see a glorious woman that I dragged into the mud. I know the blonde head prostrating on the floor that night with the weight of filth, is never going to look up again. More disgraced, dishonored, ashamed than the day before, she will slide into the darkness. That white countenance who believed in pure love, who thought she could live her life according to her principles, that woman who protected her innocence and virtue in her own selfish way . . . where are those virtues now? That chest, which used to be filled with joyful abundance like the golden chalice of deities, will forever be filled with a shameful memory; nightmares worse than death itself will be tearing it into pieces. My God! What had I done? I had forever tainted those eyes that I was ready to die for, with shame. Those eyes couldn't look at others anymore. I am such an abominable person, such a horrible sinner that I wish I could be put on public display as punishment and burn for eternity. I know now that there cannot be more unhappy, more pitiful people than sinners in this world. How I pity those sinners I used to hate and how I curse myself for thinking that I was better than them!

April 20

I had treated Macide horribly but at least she holds the right to have self-respect. What about Seviyye?

I didn't sleep at all last night. I feel so low and ashamed thinking how I taint the honor of our bedroom. Macide surely doesn't know anything. Nowadays she is so very busy with the uprisings that are eating up the country!

April 21

The Action Army is approaching. In my prostrating soul, the love of my homeland, which I thought was obliterated by my personal love affairs, remains triumphant; it heaves my generous heart. To the frontlines! For the happy future of a nation, to the frontlines! Stars are now floating across my mind, over my tainted character.

It is early in the morning. Macide is asleep. I see the peacefulness of an angel on Hikmet's little face. I will leave now! These two people whose lives I ruined will perhaps feel a victory crown on their head when I die.

Epilogue

It's a glorious, exceptional day in May. The country that was boiling over, storming, wrestling in blood for a few days is now calm and quiet! The golden rays slide from the silvery minarets of the mosque and sweep over the bowing heads of those who are humbly praying. A marvelous, harmonious voice echoes on the austere walls of the mosque, and rains on the souls of the listeners with a profound sense of reverence; a melancholic, faithful bliss. There are sobbing children and weeping women holding their handkerchiefs on their mouths. They are reciting the Koran for the Freedom Martyrs. Households with empty corners, widows, orphans each beg for a drop of consolation and forbearance from God's grace and mercy.

"Pray Fatiha for the souls of our sisters and brothers who died for the salvation of their homeland."

Thousands of heads humbled in prayer, thousands of hearts weep . . .

In the middle of the crowd is a woman, with ethereal black eyes and slim, sunken cheeks, and a blonde boy, the youngest of the orphans, who clings to her!

The woman says in a low voice: "Hikmet, my son, you should always be ready to die for things you believe in, for justice, for your homeland."

And then she adds, sobbing: "Just like, just like your father!"

The End.